I saw a film once about an alien who landed on Earth in a human body in a mental hospital. He had all this amazing stuff to teach everyone and he kept telling the doctors who he was, where he was from, and what he had to offer in the way of secrets of the universe and stuff; but they just thought he was crazy and pumped him full of drugs and he stayed there until he died. Maybe something like that happened to my dad. He wants more than anything to call us and it's been five years, and wherever he's locked up he's not allowed to phone and he's just waiting for us to find him. This sort of thought, and other variations, occur to me at least once every day.

Like I said, it's the not knowing that's hard.

Also by Jenny Valentine

Broken Soup

JENNY VALENTINE

me,
the
missing,
and the
dead

HARPER TEEN

An Imprint of HarperCollinsPublishers

For Alex and his Tardis heart

HarperTeen is an imprint of HarperCollins Publishers.

Me, the Missing, and the Dead
Text copyright © 2007 by Jenny Valentine
All rights reserved. Printed in the United States of America.
No part of this book may be used or reproduced in any manner
whatsoever without written permission except in the case of brief
quotations embodied in critical articles and reviews. For information address HarperCollins Children's Books, a division of
HarperCollins Publishers, 10 East 53rd Street, New York, NY
10022.

Library of Congress Cataloging-in-Publication Data
Valentine, Jenny.
    [Finding Violet Park]
    Me, the missing, and the dead / Jenny Valentine. — 1st
American ed.
        p.   cm.
    Originally published in Great Britain in 2007 under the title:
Finding Violet Park.
    Summary: When a series of chance events leaves him in posses-
sion of an urn with ashes, sixteen-year-old Londoner Lucas Swain
becomes convinced that its occupant, Violet Park, is communicat-
ing with him, initiating a voyage of self-discovery that forces him
to finally confront the events surrounding his father's sudden dis-
appearance.
    ISBN 978-0-06-085070-8
    [1. Death—Fiction. 2. Missing persons—Fiction. 3. Fathers—
Fiction. 4. Single-parent families—Fiction. 5. Coming of age—
Fiction. 6. London (England)—Fiction. 7. England—Fiction.]
I. Title.
PZ7.V25213Me 2008   2007014476
[Fic]—dc22   CIP
                                                 AC

Typography by Christopher Stengel
10 11 12 13 14   CG/CW   10 9 8 7 6 5 4 3 2
❖
First American paperback edition, 2010
Originally published as *Finding Violet Park* in Great Britain
in 2007 by HarperCollins*Publishers* Ltd.

Thank you thank you thank you to:

VERONIQUE BAXTER

STELLA PASKINS

GILLIE RUSSELL

JANE GRIFFITHS

BELINDA HOLLYER

PAT AND CHRIS CUTFORTH

AND THE MARVELOUS LAUREN P.

| one |

The minicab office was up a cobbled alley with little flat houses on either side. That's where I first met Violet Park, what was left of her. There was a healing center next door—a pretty upscale name for a place with a battered brown door and no proper door handle and stuck-on wooden numbers in the shape of clowns. The 3 of number 13 was a *w* stuck on sideways. I thought it was kind of sad and I liked it at the same time.

I never normally take cabs, but it was five o'clock in the morning and I was too tired to walk anywhere and I'd just found a tenner in my coat pocket. I went in for a lift home and strolled right into the weirdest encounter of my life.

It turns out the ten pounds wasn't mine at all. My sister, Mercy, had borrowed my coat the night before—

without asking—even though boys' clothes don't suit her and it was at least two sizes too big. She was livid with me about the money. I said maybe she should consider it rent and wouldn't the world be a better place if people stopped taking things that didn't belong to them?

It's funny when you start thinking about pivotal moments in your life like this, chance happenings that end up meaning everything. Sometimes, when I'm deciding which route to take to, say, the cinema in Camden, I get this feeling like maybe if I choose the wrong route, bad stuff will happen to me. This sort of thinking can make decisions really, really difficult because I'm always wondering what happens to all the choices we decide not to make. Like Mum says, as soon as she married Dad she realized she'd done the wrong thing. As she was walking back down the aisle, she could practically see her single self through the arch of the church door dancing around in the sunlight, without a care in the world, and she could have spat. I like to picture Mum, in a fancy white dress with big sticky hair, hanging on to Dad's arm and thinking about spitting on the church carpet. It always makes me smile.

Whatever. Mercy decided to borrow my coat and she

forgot to decide to remove the money. I decided to spend the whole night with my friend Ed in his posh mum's house (Miss Denmark 1979 with elocution lessons) and then I made the choice to take a cab.

It was dark in the alley, blue-black with a sheen of orange from the street lamps on the high street, almost dawn and sort of timeless. My shoes made such a ringing noise on the cobbles, I started to imagine I was back in time, in some Victorian red-light district. The mini-cab office was modern and pretty ugly. One of the three strip lights on the ceiling was blinking on and off, but the other two were working perfectly. Their over-brightness hurt my eyes and made everyone look sort of gray and pouchy and ill. There were no other customers, just bored, sleepy drivers waiting for the next fare, chain-smoking or reading three-day-old papers. There was a framed map of Cyprus on one wall and one of those heaters that they reckon are portable with a great big bottle you have to fit in the back. We had one like that in the hostel when we went on a school trip to the Brecon Beacons last year. Those things are not portable.

The dispatcher was in this little booth up a few stairs with a window looking down on the rest of them. You could tell he was the boss of the place. He had a cigar in his mouth, and the smoke was going in his eyes so he had to squint. The cigar was bouncing up and down as he talked, and you could see he thought he was Tony Soprano or someone.

Everybody looked straight at me when I walked in because I was the something happening in their boring night shift. Suddenly I felt very light-headed and my insides were going hot and cold, hot and cold. I'm tall for my age, but everyone staring up at me from their chairs made me feel like some kind of weird giant. The only person not staring at me was Tony Soprano, so I focused on him and I smiled so they'd all see I was friendly and hadn't come in for trouble. He was chomping on that cigar, working it around with his teeth and puffing away on it so hard his little booth was filling up with smoke. I thought that if I stood there long enough he might disappear from view like an accidental magic trick. The smoke forced its way through the cracks and joints of his mezzanine control tower. It was making me queasy, so I searched around, still smiling, for something else to look at.

That's when I first saw Violet. I say "Violet" but

that's stretching it because I didn't even know her name then and what I actually saw was an urn with her inside it.

The urn was the only thing in that place worth looking at. Maybe it was because I'd been up all night, maybe I needed to latch on to something in there to stop myself from passing out, I don't know—I found an urn. Halfway up a wood-paneled wall there was a shelf with some magazines and a cup and saucer on it, the sort you find in church halls and hospitals. Next to them was this urn that at the time I didn't realize was an urn. It looked like some kind of trophy or maybe full of cookies or something. It was wooden, grainy, and had a rich gloss that caught the light and threw it back at me. I was staring at it, trying to figure out what it was exactly. I didn't notice that anyone was talking to me until I caught the smell of cigar really strongly and realized that the fat dispatcher had opened his door because banging on his window hadn't got my attention.

"You haven't come for her have you?" he asked. I didn't get the joke, but everyone else did because they all started laughing at once.

Then I laughed too because everybody laughing was

funny and I said, "Who?"

The cigar bobbed down towards his chin with each syllable and he nodded towards the shelf. "The old lady in the box."

I didn't stop laughing, but really I can't remember if I thought it was funny or not. I shook my head, and because I didn't know what else to say I said, "No, I need a cab to Queens Crescent, please." A driver called Ali got up and I followed him out to his car. I walked behind him down the alley and out into the wider space of the high street.

I asked Ali what he knew about the dead woman on the shelf. He said she'd been around since before he started working there, which was eighteen months ago. Somebody had left her in a cab and never collected her. He told me if I wanted to know the whole story I should speak to the boss whose name I instantly forgot because he was always Tony Soprano to me.

The sun was coming up and the buildings with the light behind them looked like their own shadows. I thought, How could anyone end up on a shelf in a cab office for all eternity? I'd heard of purgatory, the place you wait when heaven and hell aren't that sure they want you, but I'd never thought it meant being stuck in a box in Apollo Cars forever. I couldn't get the question out of my head. I felt it burrowing down to some dark place in my skull, waiting for later.

Thinking about it now, it's all down to decision making again, you see. My better self didn't get in the cab straightaway that morning. My better self strode right back in and rescued Violet from the cigar smoke, the two-way radio, the instant coffee, and the conversation of men who should have known better than to talk like that in front of an old lady. And after liberating her from the confines of the cab office, my better self released her from her wooden pot and sprinkled her liberally over the crest and all the four corners of Primrose Hill while the sun came up.

But my real self, the disappointing one, he got in the car with Ali, gave him directions to my house, and left her there alone.

My name is Lucas Swain and I was almost sixteen when this began, the night I stayed too late at Ed's house and met Violet in her urn. Some things about me in case you're interested. I have a mum called Nick and a dad called Pete (somewhere) and a big sister called Mercy, the clothes borrower, who I've mentioned. She's about at the peak of a sarcastic phase that's lasted maybe six years already. I also have a little brother called Jed.

Here's something about Jed. On the days I take him to school, he always thinks up a funny thing to tell me. We are always at the same place when he tells me this funny thing, the last stretch once we've turned the corner into Princess Road. You can tell when Jed's thought of something early because he can't wait to get there. On the days he's struggling to come up with it, he drags his feet and we end up being late, which neither of us minds. The punch line is my brother's way of saying good-bye.

The other cool thing about Jed is that he's never met our dad and he doesn't care. Dad went missing just before Jed was born, so they've never set eyes on each other. Jed doesn't know him at all.

There's a lot of that with Dad, the not knowing. Mum puts him down for abandoning us, and I half listen and nod because it makes her feel better. But I worry that she's not being fair, because if he got hit by a bus or trapped in a burning building or dropped out of a plane, how was he supposed to let us know?

I saw a film once about an alien who landed on Earth in a human body in a mental hospital. He had all this amazing stuff to teach everyone and he kept telling the doctors who he was, where he was from, and what he had to offer in the way of secrets of the universe and stuff; but they just thought he was crazy and pumped him full of drugs and he stayed there until he died. Maybe something like that happened to my dad. He wants more than anything to call us and it's been five years, and wherever he's locked up he's not allowed to phone and he's just waiting for us to find him. This sort of thought, and other variations, occur to me at least once every day.

Like I said, it's the not knowing that's hard.

| two |

Ali dropped me off in his cab, and even though everyone was about to get up at home I went straight to bed. Mum walked past my room a couple of times in her pajamas, giving me her special "You stayed out too late" look, but I pretended not to notice.

I lay there for ages but I couldn't sleep. Jed had Saturday morning TV on too loud. Mum was singing along to something really lame on the radio. Mercy had found my coat on the stairs and was slamming doors and ranting about the money I spent getting home. But it wasn't them keeping me awake. All that's quite normal for a Saturday and I usually sleep right through. Every time I closed my eyes, the urn was there on its crappy shelf glaring at me, which was unsettling and made me open my eyes again. It was the strangest feeling, being reproached by an urn.

I got out of bed, put my clothes back on, and went for a walk on the heath. It was a beautiful day, all vast blue sky and autumn colors and a clean breeze that made me forget I hadn't slept. But I couldn't relax into it. That part of the heath is covered with enormous crows. They've got massive feet and they walk around staring at their massive feet like they can't believe how big they are. They all look like actors with their hands behind their backs, rehearsing the bit in that play when the king says, "Now is the winter of our discontent. . . ."

I watched them for a while and then I walked up to the top of kite hill and ate an apple. You can pretty much see the whole of London from up there: St. Paul's, the Telecom tower, the buildings at Canary Wharf, and the docks. There were a few runners on the athletic track just below me and plenty of dog walkers and little kids, but not many old ladies; and that set me wondering what all the old people who live in London got up to with their time.

What did the old lady in the cab office do before she did nothing all day in that urn?

Did she get up really, really early in the morning like

most old people? Mum says that's their work ethic, the same reason old men wear suits and ties instead of tracksuit bottoms and old ladies line up outside the post office half an hour before it even opens. But doesn't getting up that early just mean there are more hours to fill with being old?

Before then I'd never thought what it was actually like to be an old person. I'd just weave in and out of them on the pavement, and smirk with my friends at their funny hair and high-waisted trousers and the way they make paying for something at a checkout last for ages just to have someone to talk to. One minute the thought never crossed my mind, the next I was really and truly concerned about what it was like to be old and stuck in London, where everyone moved faster than you and even the simplest thing could end up taking all day.

It was her. I know it was. It was my old lady, the dead one in the urn.

I remember sitting there on the hill with kites whipping through the air behind me and the thought occurring to me that she and I might actually be having some kind of conversation. A dead old lady was trying to educate me about the over-sixties from her place on the shelf. It was a good feeling, a hairs-raising-on-the-back-of-your-neck feeling, like when you hear a wicked bit of music or when you're high and someone you're really into is sitting next to you. I suspected I was making it up but that hardly mattered. I make a lot of things up that are important to me, like being irresistible to girls, or being moody and mysterious like my dad, or what my dad might be up to at any moment, even this one.

| three |

I walked home the long way so I could watch what was going on. The street we live on is a good place, I think. It's a market street, fruit and veg every day, and then other things on Thursdays and Saturdays, like fresh fish and feather dusters and crap clothes and other stuff Mercy reckons is all stolen. One time one of the men from the market fell in the road and nearly got hit by his own van, and Mercy said, "Oh look, he's fallen off the back of a truck," and I laughed so hard.

The market end of the street is what my mum and her friends call the "wrong" end. I don't know when my mum became such a snob about the wrong and not-wrong ends of life. We're only here because Dad's mum and dad took pity on us when he disappeared and let us move in, and then they went into sheltered housing round the corner. Before that we lived in a dump and she wasn't snobby about stuff then.

The other interesting thing about our street is that it's called a crescent, but as far as I can make out it's actually dead straight.

We live in a whole house, which is rare nowadays in this part of London. More and more people are fitting into smaller and smaller spaces, like in New York. Mum talks a lot about selling the house and moving out of London, where she could get loads more for her money. Grown-ups spend a lot of time talking about the price of houses and how much they could add to the price of a house if they painted the kitchen terra-cotta and added a power shower. It's like they're never happy with the way things are and they think they'll be happier if the bathroom looks different. I don't know why Mum bothers with all that when she's not going anywhere.

Here's how I know.

For a start, Mum would go crazy in the country in about five minutes. Even when we went to Bath for the day to see all the Roman stuff, she kept commenting on how small-minded and provincial people were and how nobody in the countryside has any "spatial awareness."

Also Jed would miss his friends, and Mercy would throw a total tantrum and leave home to live in sin in a damp apartment with her boyfriend. I wouldn't go either without a fight.

You probably can't even get that much more for your money elsewhere; that's just something estate agents tell you because they want to get their hands on the family home.

Plus when Dad comes back we have to be here or he'll never find us.

That's what happens when someone disappears. They trap you in time. You can't change anything, not drastically, because it's the same as giving up hope. I've changed loads since he left: I've grown maybe about a meter, I shave almost every two days, and my hair is way longer too. He might not even recognize me if he did knock on the door and I answered it. But I can't help that and I'm definitely against changing anything else, just in case.

My dad was a pretty cool guy. In all the photos I've seen of him he looked good. There's no evidence of him wearing platform shoes or jackets that were two sizes too small or ridiculous sideburns, like other people's dads. He seemed to stand alone, effortlessly cool, in a room full of serious fashion errors.

Now I wear my dad's suits and shirts because they just about fit me. I wouldn't let Mum throw them out because I was expecting him back anytime. And I suppose it makes me quite proud that I'm big enough now, almost as tall as Dad was when he went, with exactly the same size feet. But it guts me too because in all the time that it's taken me to grow up, he hasn't come back.

Mum hates me wearing Dad's clothes. The first time I did it she burst into tears. She says I am already enough like he was when she first met him, and she feels sorry for the girl who's going to fall in love with me because it hasn't exactly been a picnic from her point of view.

The thing about my dad, though, he didn't just look cool, he actually was; and no amount of wearing his clothes is going to make me him, or even nearly him, ever. My dad was a journalist. I remember him as the man in the room who people wanted to be next to, the one they were interested in. I'm more like the one in the room who people forget is there.

Mum and Dad might have been in love before they

got married. I think they were having the time of their lives until Mum got pregnant with Mercy. Everyone was really upset with them for doing it without rings on their fingers, so they got married in a church before the bump that became Mercy was big enough to show. Mum says it wasn't Mercy that screwed things up, because Dad loved being a dad. It was the getting married that really pissed him off because he hated doing what he was told.

What is it about people that makes them want to get married, anyway? I don't know how anyone could ever be sure enough of something like that. I can't decide how to get to school. I can't order food in a cafeteria without spending the rest of the meal worrying I've made the wrong choice. I don't reckon I'll ever be able to do it. And on the evidence I've got, meaning my family (exhibit A: big empty space where a husband and dad used to be), I'm not sure it's even worth the bother.

And how come if Mum knew it was a bad idea the moment she'd done it, she didn't have the sense to know it a week or a day or even ten minutes earlier? I just don't get it. And when I see what Mum's left with after so many years and hear her complaining that she can't even remember loving Dad or wanting kids or whatever, it makes no sense to me at all.

It makes me determined to live life with my eyes open, even if it means making no decisions at all.

| four |

On Monday, instead of double geography and French class, I went back to the minicab office for another look at the urn. There were more people around, the shops were open on the main street, and there were some last-ditch battles for parking. Basically, a much less attractive place when awake, but the alley itself was pretty quiet. There was a lady walking up and down. The way she was walking had this strange rhythm, like four steps forward—stop—up on tiptoes—stop—three steps forward—stop; and when she got to the top of the mews she turned round and started again.

When I passed her she said, "Sorry to ask, but can you spare a cigarette?"

I said no and took my hands out of my pockets to

show her I wasn't hiding any. And I wasn't, because I might smoke weed now and again, but I would never smoke tobacco for these reasons, among others.

1. It doesn't get you high. What's the point of being addicted to something that will kill you and doesn't even make you laugh or feel good or anything?
2. It kills you.
3. It smells bad.
4. Cigarettes cost very little to make but there's a load of tax on them that goes straight to the government, making them rich. That means the people who are supposed to take care of our health and welfare and help keep the fabric of society together are making a profit out of something really addictive that doesn't get you high and will kill you. Also, I'm not old enough to vote so I'm avoiding tax generally, where I can help it.
5. Mercy told me something about the tobacco giants ripping off their farmers and paying them next to nothing. Mercy's boyfriend smokes American Spirit, which are fair trade and organic, apparently, if you can get your head round the idea of an organic cigarette.

6. Not-organic cigarettes contain about 250 poisonous toxins that will also kill you.

I stood outside Apollo Cars for a while, with the lady pacing behind me, and I tried to think about what I might say when I went in. There were those vertical venetian blinds in the window, the kind that are made out of plasticky cardboard pieces held together with cheap chains made of tiny ball bearings. The blinds were really dirty, but I liked the way they cut up the view inside, as if somebody got a photo of a minicab office out of a magazine and cut it into strips. If I took a step to the right I could see the urn on its shelf, and if I moved back to where I was it disappeared from view and I could see somebody's profile and the front page of two different newspapers. The urn looked so precious in there compared to everything else, so completely out of place.

Anyone walking into the alley just then would have seen a lady with a demented walk and a boy hopping from one foot to the other, and would most probably have turned round and walked back out again.

As soon as I went in I knew I hadn't really thought

this thing through. I was way underprepared. I could hear my blood shushing through my ears like a pulse. For a start, I'd been standing outside for longer than I realized, arousing suspicion. Tony Soprano was halfway down his stairs already. Whether he remembered me from the other night or not, he had every right to think I was nuts. I was hovering on the spot, smiling like an idiot. And anyway, paying a call on the remains of a dead stranger isn't the sanest thing I've ever tried to do.

He asked me if I wanted a cab and I said no, and then when he turned his back to me I changed my mind and said yes, and he laughed and asked if I had any money, which I didn't. Then he told me to leave, which wasn't the cleverest time to ask him about the dead lady. He walked right up to me then, sallow with gray bags under his eyes and cigar breath.

This, as far as I can remember it, is the conversation I had with Tony Soprano.

Me: Why have you got a dead lady's ashes?

TS: What's it to you?

Me: Is she yours?

TS: What? (*looks at colleagues*) What a question!

Me: I mean, did you know her? Was she a relative or something?

TS: No.

Me: What are you going to do with her?

TS: Who? None of your business, mate.

Me: Well—

TS: When they collect her they can do whatever they want.

Me: Who?

TS: The family, whoever left her; who d'you think?

Me: Are they going to?

TS: No idea. You're not touching it. Get that idea out of your head right now.

Me: What's her name?

TS: (*staring at me hard for the count of five and sighing*) If I tell you, will you leave?

Me: Yes.

TS: (*picking up the urn and showing me the metal plaque on the side that reads VIOLET PARK 1927–2002*) Now get out.

It was like a light going on in my brain.

I read once in a comic about readiness potential. It's the way your brain is always one step ahead of you, even though you think you're the one in charge. It's pretty complicated, but I think I understand it and it goes like this.

First you have to get the difference between action and reaction.

Action is throwing a ball and reaction is dodging out of the way when you suddenly realize that the ball's going to hit you.

Your brain is firing signals all the time, telling you to scratch your nose or smile or put one foot in front of the other when you're walking. But some things you do, like blink or drop a hot piece of toast, you couldn't possibly know you were going to do beforehand because you didn't see them coming. That's when your brain proves it knows everything before you do, because it has to send the signal and the signal takes time.

This is called the readiness potential, the way your brain tells your body what to do before even you know you need to do it.

And what reminded me of the readiness potential

thing was that when I read Violet's name, I realized I knew it after all, before he showed it to me, even though there was no way I could. I heard it in my head just before I saw it written down, like when you watch a film and the dubbing's out of sync, so you hear what people say a bit before their mouths move. Right then I was pretty wired about it. I was thinking about that conversation-with-a-dead-old-person feeling I'd had on the hill, and I was sure that the only way I could have known her name was that she'd already told me.

It flew around in my brain like a pigeon trapped in a building, flitting through the spaces, clattering against the sides. *V-I-O-L-E-T*. A good strong name, a name that's a color—and there aren't many of those around—and also a flower, soft and pretty and old-fashioned, the perfect name for a dead old lady.

It was all I could do to stop myself from grabbing the urn and running off. I felt like I was her only hope at that moment. She'd been dead long enough to know there was no one coming for her. It still makes me sick to think of her stuck there since I was eleven, the same time as my dad went wherever.

Tony Soprano put Violet back on the shelf. I'd

promised to leave, and he was going to hold me to it. To stay calm on the way out I made a list in my head of all the good reasons to make friends with a dead lady in an urn.

1. A dead old lady would never be judgmental or lecture me like every other female on the planet.
2. If I decided to find out about her, she might turn out to be the coolest, most talented, bravest person I'd ever heard of, and I might sort of get to know her without the hassle of her actually existing.
3. I would get to rescue her, and I never did that for anyone before. It sort of makes you need them, too, in your own way.
4. A dead old lady would be easy to like because she couldn't leave any more than she had already.

I do know, I am aware, that a boy my age should have thought more about bringing home a living girl than a dead old lady. And I did care about that other stuff, about girls and sex and stuff; I'm not a total freak. It's just that Violet was becoming my newest friend, and she was working her way to the front of my brain all the time, like new friends do.

If you think about it, a person being dead isn't any barrier to finding out what they are like. Half the people we learn about in school have been dead for ages. People write whole books about William Blake and Henry VIII and Marilyn Monroe and they've never met them, and they still sound like they know what they are talking about.

I met Violet after she died but it didn't stop me from getting to know her. What I keep trying to prove is that I'm not as insane as I'm sounding.

| five |

Of all the places I would like to be when I'm dead, Apollo Cars is the last. I can't decide what my first choice is yet, but my top three places so far for being quiet and on my own (which sounds like a good description of being dead if you think about it) are as follows.

1. Primrose Hill—over the top and down again to the quiet side. It doesn't have a great view like at the top, but it is peaceful and for some reason hardly anyone goes there, even on days when the park is mobbed. Also, it's where my dad's old friend Bob had a tree planted to celebrate when Jed was born.
2. St. Pancras Church—I don't like cemeteries in a Goth way because actually, apart from Violet, I'm not that comfortable with dead people. But I do like St.

Pancras. Mary Shelley, who wrote *Frankenstein*, used to be buried there next to her mum, who died giving birth to her; but then I think they got moved to St. Albans, which is another thing you wouldn't expect to do when you're dead.

The church is on a gentle hill and you can't see the cemetery from the road or the beauty of the place really until you're right inside it. There's a tree there called the Hardy Tree with loads of old gravestones leaned up against it. It's called the Hardy Tree after Thomas Hardy, the famous writer who invented that place Wessex and made up sad stories about beautiful milkmaids and other pessimistic country people. He's not buried there and he wasn't even famous when he had anything to do with the Hardy Tree. He was actually an engineer, I think, and he was in charge of clearing the way for the railway line out to the Midlands. He had to shrink the cemetery to make room and squish all the dead bodies into a smaller place. He might even have been the one who moved Mary Shelley and her mum. There must have been a bit of a mix-up or something, because the headstones of some of the people who got moved just got left up against the tree.

I wonder how big the tree was then because it's pretty old now. Then I wonder how big Jed's tree on Primrose Hill will be in two hundred years, and I wonder if anyone will find out about it and call it the Swain Tree, because maybe Jed will be famous for something one day.

3. The City on a Sunday. Dad used to take me. There's no one there. You can walk around and pretend you're in one of those science fiction stories, like *The Day of the Triffids* or *48 Hours Later*. All the modern buildings reek of money and bad taste; and you can still feel the frantic stuff that goes on all week long, almost like the ghost of it is there on a Sunday, like the place is just exhausted with the pace of it all. And there are these really, really old bits, too, all mixed in. You can be standing at some super modern glass box with your back to the oldest pub in London, and round the corner there's a really narrow little lane called Wardrobe Street, where they really did used to make wardrobes in about 17-something. It's like time travel, street to street, and that's a brilliant thing.

* * *

I didn't know what Violet's places might be, where she liked to spend her time, where she'd want to end up. It's a sad thing for nobody to know about a person. Before I die I'm going to leave strict instructions about where I want to spend the rest of time. I hope I won't be so completely alone in the world that no one will remember to collect me after my funeral. It's like those stories in the local paper about people who die and nobody notices for weeks. Then they start smelling, and suddenly their neighbors remember they haven't seen them for ages. Whenever I think about anyone living or dying all by themselves I end up thinking about my dad and wondering if he died alone, and if he thought about us when he died. Or I wonder if he is alive and ever thinks about us now.

I've only ever been to two funerals. The first one was my grandad's—my mum's dad—and I don't remember it because I was about two, but Mum says I spent the whole time crawling around and barking like a dog.

The second one was for this girl in my class called Angelique, and she died when we were twelve. She went to somewhere like Spain with her mum and dad and died in the shower of carbon monoxide poisoning. They flew her home and the whole class went to her funeral. We all wanted to go because she was popular and a nice person and everyone was upset that she wasn't ever coming back.

She was in a coffin made of bamboo or wicker or something, like a beautiful Angelique-shaped basket covered in pink blossoms. On either side of her there were silver buckets filled with sand and flowers. You got a candle when you came in and you lit it and put it in a bucket, so there were maybe a hundred candles surrounding her. The light was sort of eerie and full of life.

When the priest talked about commending Angelique to heaven, the flowers in some of the buckets all seemed to catch fire at the same time and you could hear this gasp go round the church like it was a sign or something, and nobody wanted to put the fires out. When Angelique's dad went to pick up the coffin on the way out, he leaned against it for support, like he was hugging her, and that really got to me.

After the funeral, back at Angelique's house, we had this kind of circle-time thing where we all said something we liked about Angelique or told a funny story about her. They make you do circle time at school a lot when something bad happens, or sometimes just because they want to. It can be OK, or pretty crap, depending; but that circle time at Angelique's was just about the most touching thing ever. Everybody had something they really wanted to say, and Angelique's mum and dad were crying and laughing at the same time. You could see they were going to get by on those stories for years to come.

I doubt Violet's funeral was much to write home about, seeing as she was the guest of honor and got left in a taxi. I doubt there was a circle time for her.

If we ever find my dad and he's dead, I'm going to organize the biggest funeral you've ever seen, and I'll personally see to it that the flowers catch fire. We'll play the best music, and everyone he ever knew and liked will be there and cry their eyes out and say really nice things about him. Afterwards, back at our house, we'll have the best wake and nobody will want to leave. They'll look after Mum and make sure she's OK. They'll phone her every week instead of being too embarrassed to say anything or ever call because there isn't a body and they're a bit busy with work and they were his friends really, not hers.

* * *

When Dad first went missing there was a big, big fuss. It wasn't just Mum running around pulling her hair out (eight-and-a-half-months pregnant) and the police showing up all the time, and Mercy yelling, slamming doors, and sleeping with whoever'd have her. For a while everyone was interested, and he was all over the papers and the TV for weeks. There was this same photo of him everywhere. None of us can stand to look at it now. First because it reminds us of everything going wrong, and second because he looks so damn happy in it and that must have been an act.

I remember the exact moment Mum realized he had actually disappeared and wasn't just somewhere sleeping things off for longer than usual or stuck in the office on a deadline without calling, which often happened. I can see her now, rubbing her massive belly with this weird sort of half smile that she wore practically the whole time she was pregnant with Jed. She answered the phone and then turned suddenly to dust. I was sitting at the kitchen table, waiting for Dad to come home so there would be another boy in the house, and I was watching her. She was really beautiful when she picked up the phone—in

my memory she sort of glows and the lighting is soft—
but by the time she put it down, maybe two-and-a-half
minutes later, she was gray and old and looked like she
was going to throw up.

(She did, all night and the next day. They had to take
her to the hospital because she wasn't keeping anything
down, she hadn't slept, and everyone was worried about
the baby.)

The phone call was from a friend of Dad's at *The
Times* called Nigel Moon, who said the police had found
our car in a field somewhere in Hampshire. He asked if
Dad's passport was at home or was there a chance he had
it with him. Nigel thought she should know. He got to
her about five minutes before the police, because while
she was throwing up in the downstairs bathroom there
was a knock on the door and it was them. (Dad's passport was in a drawer upstairs, next to Mum's.)

After the big, big fuss there was nothing. In a few
weeks people began to get bored or forget. They drifted
away and left us to our own private chaos. Mum had
Jed and they both cried a lot in her room, Mercy
stopped speaking for maybe three months, and I walked
around lost and got into a lot of fights.

There's a definite stigma attached to you when someone in your family goes missing like that. A big question mark, a skeleton in your closet, a dirty shadow. In the beginning when everyone was all keen and interested, they actually didn't care at all. They were just looking for something nasty, for Dad's guilty secrets, for the cracks in our family that must have opened into massive caverns and swallowed him whole.

Was he having an affair? Was he mixed up in anything illegal? Was he murdered? Did we do it? Did he kill himself? Why? Was he having an affair? And round and round like a dog chasing its own tail until we put the telly in the cupboard and took the batteries out of the radio and stopped looking at newspapers or answering the door or going out.

Every so often now something comes out about Dad in the paper, mostly on a weekend, in the magazine, or buried in the review section. I think the name "Pete Swain" must be on a kind of reserve list of the missing, because he resurfaces every now and again, part of a roster for writers with nothing to do. In a way, going missing like that does make a good story, whoever you are. Mum says journalists like nothing better than a question with no answers, because they can never be wrong and that makes them look good. She says they're all vultures circling an old corpse. Because they mostly abandoned us when they lost the scent, she refuses to talk to any of them, even if some of them were still at school when he went missing and have nothing to feel bad about.

Only one of Dad's friends stayed friends with us after he went. Mercy says the only reason he did it was because he'd always fancied Mum and he wanted to get into her pants, but I reckon loads of good things get done for that reason and it doesn't make them any less good. He's the one who planted a tree on Primrose Hill because he thought that, even though Jed was born at such a terrible time, we shouldn't forget to celebrate. Mum made him Jed's godfather after that.

His name is Bob Cutforth, and he and Dad started out together at some local paper or other. For a while he was one of the big correspondents for the BBC, and he went all over the world and into danger zones and interviewed tyrants and dodged bullets. But then he turned out to be a really sick alcoholic and lost his job and his house and his wife. Now he lives in a studio in Kilburn, gets benefits, and writes in his notebooks all day. Still, he's never forgotten Jed's birthday even once.

| six |

If I was working in one of those swanky Soho ad agencies and I was doing consumer profiling, like where you divide people into groups according to what trousers they wear and if they're ever likely to buy fish fingers from the freezer compartment, this is how I'd profile my mum.

Age: 35–45
Sex: female
Height: 1.7 meters
Weight: 50–60 kilograms, depending
Annual income: under £15,000
Profession: classroom assistant. Sometimes she says she'd like to spend a whole week just talking to grown-ups and not wiping anybody's

nose, but the job fits in with Jed's school day
and she likes it mostly.

Status: married (estranged probably)

On the stereo: old stuff. Some of it I like. Some
of it is diabolical.

Leisure activities: walking on the heath,
swimming at the outdoor pool (summer only),
reading, knitting, learning to sew, yoga,
aggressive cleaning

If I was working at an ad agency I don't think I'd go crazy about someone like my mum. I might halfheartedly throw a few bath oils or cleaning products or hair dye her way, but she wouldn't have much to spend, so I wouldn't waste too much effort.

This would be my big mistake.

My mum is buying stuff all the time.

If there's a bogus new miracle product on the TV, me and Mercy place bets on how long before Mum buys it. Our bathroom cupboard is spilling over with twenty-four-hour moisturizers, antiwrinkle creams, cellulite busters, and hair thickeners.

Mum says she used to be a beautiful woman, but

having three kids and an absent husband has ruined her looks. She says that it's harder than you'd think to have looks and then lose them. Mercy says she should try just being ugly all her life, and that's no picnic. Mum says Mercy has low self-esteem.

The main thing about my mum is that she's sad. Life isn't turning out for her the way it was supposed to. She blames Dad for a lot of it, of course, his old friends and us; and also she blames herself.

I know this for a fact, not because she ever told me but because she told Bob Cutforth. A lot. Whenever he came over for dinner they would get wasted together and I would listen outside the kitchen door because when people are wasted they talk about stuff they can't talk about when they are sober. Once I heard Mum say to Bob that she'd spent the last year they were together hoping Dad would disappear off the face of the earth because she couldn't stand how things were between them. She said she'd wanted to be free from the job of loving him because he made it such hard work. In her fantasy of being on her own she blossomed (Mum's word) and did all the things she'd always blamed Dad for stopping her doing. But in reality, when he disappeared, she was less than she'd been before, not more.

Remembering that conversation is like being there listening to it for the first time. The line of my spine feels caught, like I need to stretch it, and my stomach is a hole. I'm listening to my own breathing and the big wall clock in the hall, and I'm staring at the streaks and blisters in the paint on the kitchen door and thinking I might kick it down and punch my mum in the face for wishing my dad away.

They're quiet for a bit, and then Bob says to her, "You didn't make him go, Nicky. What did you do? You loved him and you loved his kids. You've done nothing wrong."

Mum started crying then, just softly; and I went upstairs to my room and thought about what it was like to be her, and if her and Bob would end up getting married.

Another time, when I was sitting right there with them at the table, she said to Bob, "I wasn't as good a wife as you all thought I was, you know." Then she went on about how much she hated being stuck at home with the kids and how she resented Dad's great job. She said how she made him pay all the time and was insanely jealous and always thought he was playing around, and how she was basically never happy at what turned out to be the happiest time of her life. Bob said she shouldn't talk about that stuff in front of me, and she said, "Lucas is nearly thirteen and his dad's left us, so he's the man of the house now." Then she ruffled my hair and told me to go to bed, like I was eight, which pissed me off because I was a man when it suited her and a kid when it didn't.

She's better now than she was then.

But the thing about my mum that still bothers me is that people mostly feel sorry for her and she lets them. Mum reckons life dealt her a bad hand, which is a good way of saying that her absent husband, her three kids, and the fact that she's not twenty-one anymore are not her fault. I want to ask her if women in places like Sudan or Palestine or Kosovo worry as much about face cream and stretch marks and living without a man around, but I haven't yet, and who knows, maybe they do.

And sometimes Mum gets angry with the wrong people—meaning those who are still here as opposed to he who has left. Some days I know as soon as I look at her that I'm not going to get a civil word out of Mum at all. Even just the sound of our voices makes her roll her eyes and tut and act like we're squatters in her actual brain and not people with as much right to be and speak as she has. On a bad day like that you can tell she's programmed herself just to say NO to everything, practically before she's heard it, which means she loses out when we're saying, "Do you want anything from the shop?" or offering to put the dinner on.

What I think on days like that is this.

Maybe life didn't turn out the way Mum planned, but it's not our fault. Unless the thing we did wrong was being born; and if you start from there you can never do anything right, no matter how hard you try.

| seven |

One good side effect of Violet turning me on to old people was I got to know my gran a lot better. Her name is Pansy—another perfect name for an old lady, another flower name. I'd never really had much time for her before, what with her being old and having false teeth she got too small for, and skin like a bit of screwed-up gray tissue that you find in your coat pocket and pretty extreme opinions on just about everything. She and my grandad live round the corner in sheltered housing. Pansy says there's nothing more patronizing or that fills her with more dread than primary-color shutters. She says it's a sign that whoever lives there is no longer taken seriously. It's worth remembering that they gave up their big house to move here so that we could live in it. Pansy would rather we didn't forget it.

Pansy is a live wire. She'll talk about anything and has theories about stuff she's hardly heard of, like jungle music, PlayStation, and Internet dating. She swears all the time; but she never actually says the word, just mouths it with her face screwed up, her gums and false teeth colliding slightly, the insides of her mouth sticking together and then pulling apart so swearing becomes this strange, spongy, clacking sound. It's quite effective.

Pansy is passionate about football and has been for years. But somehow, at the same time, she's managed to learn absolutely nothing about the rules. She once said that footballers should get extra points for hitting the post or the crossbar because it's much harder than scoring a proper goal. She's a Tottenham fan because she grew up in Enfield and her dad played in the brass band at White Hart Lane. If you ask me, there's never enough reason to be a Spurs fan, because I'm into Arsenal and so was my dad. Pansy says Dad only supported Arsenal to annoy her when he was a kid. Grandad, who can take football or leave it, rolls his eyes and says, "They used to fight like cat and dog when games were on." She loves to insult Arsenal, and mostly that's fine because we're at the top of the league and they're going down.

Pansy was the first person I told about Violet. I needed to tell someone that a dead lady was talking to me, and I had several good reasons for letting her in on it. For a start, it was Violet who made me more interested in the person inside Pansy's old body. Also, I figured Violet would appreciate having another old lady around after all those cab drivers. And I knew Pansy'd be into it because she was always reading about the occult and she liked mediums and stuff. She even went to see one once to see if she could find out if Dad had "passed over," so I knew she'd never dismiss the idea of communicating with the dead.

Of course, that's the other thing that me and my gran have in common, apart from Violet and the football—my dad, her son. "Our missing link" she calls him. Mum says however bad it feels to us that Dad just went off without a word of warning, we should times it by ten for Pansy because she's his mum and mums just don't expect their kids to go before they do. So Pansy loves it when I come round, firstly because she says I'm her favorite (based purely on the fact that I look like her son and wear his clothes) and secondly because she can talk about Dad till she's run out of air and I won't lose interest.

I don't think Grandad is much help with all that. His name is Norman, and he fought in the war in North Africa, driving munitions trucks through the desert and smoking roll-up cigarettes and wetting his pants. Norman is a really nice bloke, and he's always been a good grandad; but these days he doesn't know his arse from his elbow. He's had these tiny strokes, and every time he has one (you wouldn't notice if he was having one right in front of you, they're that small), some of his memory gets wiped. Some days he's better than others, but it drives Pansy mad because she says she never knows where she is with him. One minute he's getting all romantic on her, the next he thinks she's the help come to give things a vacuum.

Pansy has a dog called Jack (Russell), and sometimes I have no idea if she's talking about the dog or Grandad.

"He's been under my feet all day and his breath smells terrible." (dog)

"He's not *been* for three days. I think he needs a good walk." (Norman)

On a good day Norman will remember that I'm Lucas, and on a stroke day he'll think I'm my dad. Me and Pansy just agreed to let it slide on stroke days because it makes him happy. Pansy says she wishes she could have a stroke so she could forget her only child had abandoned his family and headed for the hills. Then she dabs her crumpled eyes with a crumpled tissue and says, "Fffck it, let's have another slice of cake."

The times I do sit down to have a chat with Norman he's overjoyed because he doesn't otherwise get a word in edgewise most of the time and he's actually got quite a lot to say. When you first meet him and Pansy, she's the one who grabs you because she's so vibrant, sharp, energetic, and into everything. But after a while you realize that Norman is the tortoise to her hare and that if you just give him a minute, he can be very interesting and knowledgeable about a lot of things.

The person who really likes being with Norman is Jed. Jed's too young to realize that Norman forgets things. He thinks he's just doing it to be funny, and he gets a big kick out of it. Jed thinks Norman is the funniest man alive. They hang out together in the kitchen eating cookies and making model airplanes, and they laugh themselves sick over old Laurel and Hardy films. They're also allowed to take the dog out together, which is about the only time for both of them that they get to go anywhere without a responsible adult. Jed says being with Grandad is just like being with one of his friends from school except better because Grandad knows a lot more and is really good at sharing.

A while ago I got this idea in my head that Norman knew something really vital about where Dad is except he couldn't tell us because he'd forgotten. I was convinced that everything he said, however ordinary, was actually a hidden clue and if I broke the code I'd save my dad. Sometimes when he's talking to me I still cross my fingers that it will just slip out, an address or a phone number or a last message, but things are never that simple.

When I told Pansy about Violet, I did it just like I would if I'd met anyone normal, or at least alive. Violet was still on the shelf at Apollo Cars when I did it.

I think I said, "Gran, I met someone you'd really like the other night," and Pansy said something sharp like, "Well don't go getting her pregnant," and I nearly spat my biscuit out at the thought and said, "No, no, she's an old girl like you!"

"How old?" said Pansy. "Where did you meet an old lady? What do you want an old girlfriend for?"

I said, "She's in her seventies like you and she's not my girlfriend and I met her in a cab office last Friday night on my way home."

Pansy pursed her lips tight and sucked air in like she was smoking an invisible cigarette that didn't taste good. She said, "Mercy said you pinched her money, you bloody cheapskate."

"Yeah, well, I didn't," I said, and then she sort of waved her hand around to say "Let's not talk about that" and said, "What's a seventy-year-old woman doing in a cab office on a Friday night?", which was the question I'd been waiting for.

"She was on a shelf," I said a bit too quickly, and Pansy glared at me.

"Have you been smoking that wacky baccy again, Lucas?"

I glared back. "Gran, you know that's not really relevant."

"Don't use those long words with me," Pansy said. "I told your dad about that stuff and look where he is now."

I kept looking at her and I said, "Dad could be any-where, we don't know; but Violet is trapped on a shelf in a minicab office, and she needs our help."

It felt like one of those things people say in films, and it was coming out of my mouth.

"Where's Violet? What in hell are you talking about, Peter?" Norman said, and he made me jump because I'd forgotten he was there.

"I thought you were asleep," I said.

Pansy winked at me and whispered, "Sometimes it's hard to tell the difference." And then she yelled, "Nothing, Norman! Go back to sleep. It was the TV," which was a bare-faced lie because the TV wasn't even on. Then we were back to the film script and she said, "Is there a ransom?"

It wasn't quite what I was expecting. "What?"

"If someone's holding an old lady hostage in a cab office, they must be doing it for a reason."

"She's dead, Gran," I said, and I counted to ten for it to sink in.

"They've got a dead lady on a shelf? That's disgusting!" Pansy was overexcited. I could see the little explosions happening behind her eyes. "How did you meet her if she was dead, Lucas?"

"She's in an urn. She's been cremated."

Pansy didn't say anything to that. She just unclasped her hands, fingers spread out on either side of her face, still trying to catch the answer to her last question. Her eyebrows were raised so high up her face that her forehead looked like a terraced hillside. I knew I had her full attention. Now I just had to reel her in.

"Gran, I'm not promising anything, but I think she's communicating with me from . . ."

Pansy mouthed the words at me in a furious display of facial gymnastics, "*The other side?*"

I nodded and went to put the kettle on.

I did this because I know that my grandparents' response to anything, from the disappearance of their son to the commercials in the middle of their favorite soap, is to make a cup of tea. I don't think they've ever gone more than an hour or two without one in fifty years. They are tea junkies.

And maybe there's some truth in their tea beliefs. Once she'd had a sip, Pansy was back to her normal self, no more gawping and tonguing her teeth back and forth. She was all helpful hints and great ideas.

I said I wanted to rescue Violet. The rest of the plan was mostly down to Pansy.

It was brilliant and simple.

The first thing to do was phone Apollo Cars.

"If I don't know the answer to any of his questions, I'll just tell him I don't remember. Nobody gives an old lady a hard time," Pansy said. Then she dialed the number and started mewing into the receiver in her old-lady voice. This always gets me because you'd think an old lady wouldn't be able to do a good old-lady impression, but Pansy can.

"Hello? Mr. Soprano?" she said, and I waved NO at her but it didn't register. "Have you got my sister there?"

Then she said, "Maybe I've got the wrong cab office. She's been mislaid. Her name is Violet, and she's in an urn. Ring any bells?"

I could hear his tinny, squashed voice from where I was sitting but I couldn't work out what he was saying.

"Well, I am sorry you've been stuck with her all this time; I've been abroad you see." She said "abroad" like she imagined the queen would and arched her see-through old eyebrows at me.

I had to leave the room then because Norman had woken up and was misbehaving in the kitchen. Norman and the dog scoff chocolate together behind Pansy's back. It's like she's running a prisoner-of-war camp and him and Private Jack Russell have got contraband. She says she wouldn't mind except that they both do it until they're sick. She says Norman doesn't remember how much he's had and the dog just takes advantage.

I took the chocolate off Norman and let the dog out; and when I got back, Pansy was wrapping things up. She was blowing her nose in a fresh pink tissue and sounding all teary, the old faker ("It's very kind of you, Mr. Soprano, to go to so much trouble . . . Only if you're sure . . . I can't thank you enough," etc., etc.). Then she banged the phone down with a smile. The thing about false teeth is that they don't match your face. Pansy looks like she's borrowed someone else's grin, some famous actor—George Clooney's perfect Hollywood pearlies stuck in the middle of her collapsing face.

"He's coming," she said, "in half an hour, in person, to hand her over."

"Well, I'd better go, then," I said, getting my coat and trying to maneuver past Norman, who was in the doorway and wasn't sure if he was on his way in or on his way out.

"Lucas Swain, you get your arse back in here!" Pansy said.

"He can't see me, Gran. If he sees me he won't let you have her."

"Well, hide in the bedroom, then. I'm letting a stranger in here for your benefit. The least you can do is be on hand."

So I hid in Pansy and Norman's bedroom for twenty-four minutes and I worried about what might go wrong.

- The urn would get dropped and burst open.
- The urn would roll around on the backseat of the car and burst open.
- Soprano would crash the car, get a concussion, and forget about the urn entirely.
- He'd just lied to get an old lady off the phone and had no intention of coming over.
- Pansy had given him the wrong address.
- Pansy had forgotten to give him an address at all.
- Norman would open the door and say "No thank you" or "You've got the wrong house" and shut it again.
- Norman would think the ashes were my dad and lose it completely.

- Norman would think the ashes were Pansy and lose it completely.
- Norman would blow Pansy's story by saying very loudly she never had a sister called Violet.
- Pansy would call Violet the name of one of her real sisters (Dolly, Daisy, Daphne, Delia—I don't know what happened with Pansy. They must have run out of *D*s).
- Pansy and Norman would fall asleep and not hear the doorbell (quite common).
- One or all of these things would force me out of hiding so Soprano would see me before the drop.

After twenty-four minutes the doorbell rang. Pansy heard it and answered it. She'd done herself up a bit with makeup, a cardigan, and some pearls. I watched through a crack in the door. Tony Soprano carried the urn very carefully. He put Violet on the mantelpiece next to the photo of my dad and said how sorry he was about Pansy's sister. Then Norman in a random piece of brilliance came out with "She's dead you know," and they probably nodded gravely or something because it was very quiet.

Tony Soprano must have seen a picture of Pansy and her real dead sister Dolly, who's also on the mantelpiece, because he said, "Is this her?" and Pansy said, "Yes, she was a real live wire," and Norman said, "You can say that again; she was anyone's, your big sister." Tony Soprano sort of coughed, and then said he really should be going. Pansy walked him to the door (about a meter) and said good-bye; and I thought what a decent bloke he was really, taking it all so seriously and being respectful and doing the right thing.

Then I came out of the bedroom because Soprano had gone and Pansy was having a go at Norman for calling her big sister a slut. I wasn't sure how Violet would feel in this new place in front of arguing strangers.

She was resting on the mantelpiece to the right and slightly behind the old front-page photo of my dad. They sat there together. I stared at them from one of Pansy's over-fussy armchairs and wondered for a minute what we'd done. Was it really any of my business where a set of ashes ended up? Was I out of my mind the night I set my heart on rescuing her?

I could feel Pansy's eyes going from me to the urn, waiting for something to happen, maybe a disembodied voice or my eyes to roll back in my head, or a power cut and some ectoplasm. I didn't want to let her down.

Then . . . I felt it, faint at first but unmistakable.

Violet was happy.

She was warm (heating on constantly) and she liked the decor (overcrowded and a lot of crochet) and nobody was smoking or swearing. She wanted a bit of music on. Rachmaninov's Fourth (which, by the way, I'd never heard of, I swear; but Norman had it on vinyl and we cranked it up. Violet knew it like the back of her hand, and she went all tingly, which was pretty amazing). Maybe sheltered accommodation in Kentish Town wasn't her first choice for eternal idyll, but it was a step up from Apollo Cars and Violet wanted us to know she was grateful.

I was bombed. My legs were shaking. Pansy thought I was the new Uri Geller. She kept staring at me with her mouth open, her teeth slipping, and a new respect in her eyes.

(For the record, I think Uri Geller is a big crazy fake, but Pansy thinks he's the real deal because Norman's watch was broken and Uri fixed it through the TV apparently.)

I decided that Violet Park and Dad weren't that different. One was dead and one was missing; but everyone has their secrets, don't they? Take any family and there'll be unspeakable stuff rattling around behind the scenes, guaranteed. Here's some of mine.

1. There's Dad (obviously), who has some other life that we know nothing about or is dead, which he's kept pretty secret, too.

2. Pansy had a kid (my dad) by an encyclopedia salesman before she married Norman. She was brave about it then, but now she won't have it mentioned and she fakes her wedding anniversaries just to make it all legit.

3. Norman couldn't have kids (mumps), but he doesn't know that we all know he's not strictly related to us. Mum told me and Mercy a long time ago, before Dad went, and I remember thinking that it made no difference. Jed doesn't know yet, at least I don't think he does. Maybe even Norman's forgotten that he's not my dad's real dad, what with missing him so much and going senile and everything.

4. Mum has had a boyfriend for over six months and

she thinks none of us know. It's not Bob (pity), but she did sleep with Bob a few times—another thing she thinks we never knew about. Mum's boyfriend is called David, and he teaches life drawing at the community center. He's nice enough, but he wears weird jewelry and talks quite a lot of crap.

5. Mercy's on the pill and she smokes and she does drugs and she shoplifts and she bunks off and she climbs out the bedroom window to visit her dealer jailbird boyfriend when she's grounded.

6. Jed wets the bed but he made Mum promise not to tell us.

7. Mum told us.

That's not even all of them, but I'm not telling any more because the point is, we've got loads of secrets and so has everybody. By my reckoning, being missing and being dead, like Dad and Violet, are just ways of keeping another, bigger secret. And secrets are never that hard to unearth. Somebody always slips up, or leaves a trail, or says the wrong thing at the right time. And then everybody finds out the truth, whether they want to or not.

| eight |

Bob Cutforth was a man with secrets. He used to have a mountain of them, and now he doesn't have any. He says that it's better this way, but it must have been pretty painful getting found out again and again, like he did, and losing everything bit by bit. The thing I really like about Bob, my absolute favorite thing about him, is that he is way happier now with nothing than he ever was before. Bob says it's the best kind of freedom, having nothing to lose.

He says that when he lived in a big house in Camden Square, with a beautiful academic wife, a sexy assistant, a pedigree dog and an impressive wine cellar, a great job and a fat wallet, he never for one minute stopped worrying. Bob worried about being robbed or murdered. His wife was neurotic and his assistant was insatiable, so he couldn't please either of them and he worried about that. His dog was on Prozac and threw herself through a plate glass window one morning when he was leaving for the airport because she didn't like being left.

Bob's job frightened the life out of him. He went to Rwanda, Afghanistan, Pakistan, the Philippines, Libya, and Colombia at times when other people were frightened just to see them on TV. No wonder he was scared. Bob says he was drinking a liter of vodka a day by the end and that the wine cellar was just for show.

I suppose the other big thing about Bob is that he could have easily gone missing too, but he chose to stay. One minute he was everybody's hero and the next he was a degenerate sicko with no morals, no job, a mistress, a coke habit, an expensive divorce, and a drunk-driving ban. He must have been tempted to run for it; but he stuck it out, all of it, and you've got to love him for that.

I can't help wondering what was so bad that Dad couldn't face? I don't like where things go when I try to answer that question. I've said it before—it's the not knowing that drives you mad. It's the imagining things that you wish you couldn't think up all by yourself.

Of course, Bob is the best person for talking about

my dad, and he knows lots of brilliant, secret stuff that kids me into thinking I know him better. Bob and my dad go back years. They worked on a local paper together when they were just out of college—*The Radnorshire Express*. Bob says there was nothing express about it. It was the slowest, dullest place he's ever lived, and if it wasn't for my dad he'd have gone off his head with boredom. I imagine it was a bit like Andover, which is the most boring place I've ever been. My mum sent me there on an adventure weekend, and I still say she should have got them for false advertising.

According to Bob my dad went missing before.

He was twenty-three or twenty-four. He was going out with a nurse from Brazil called Luzmira (Bob said it means "look at the light"). Bob and my dad were working at the *Evening Standard*, and they spent a lot of time drinking and playing serious poker with some doctors from Charing Cross Hospital. A weird crowd, Bob said, real freaks; they put him off medics for good. Bob said Dad was in over his head and owed them a load of money. Then suddenly Dad stopped coming to work or to poker, and he lost his job. Luzmira and the doctors said they hadn't seen him. His landlady put all his stuff in a cupboard and rented his room out. Bob thought Dad was dead. About three months later Dad came back, out of the blue, and he wouldn't tell anybody where he'd been, not even Bob, and he never did.

Still, if my dad can disappear and then show up once, he can do it again.

Agatha Christie went missing for a while when she was pretty famous and then she came back, but nobody knows where she went. Except my friend Ed, the one whose house I was at the night I met Violet, who reckons he knows exactly. Ed says that his great-grandfather on his mother's side was having a secret affair with Agatha Christie in Jamaica or Antigua or somewhere; but it didn't work out, so he went back to his wife in Swindon. He kept this shawl Agatha Christie had given him in his sock drawer and stroked it lovingly every now and then when his wife wasn't looking. But of course she knew, because wives in those days put their husbands' clean socks away and didn't say anything about affairs or lovers' trinkets to avoid the shame.

If my dad was holed up with a thriller writer in the West Indies (or a nurse in Brazil), my mum would kick up a stink. She is way beyond worrying about what the neighbors might say.

| nine |

I thought it would be simple once we'd got Violet out of the cab office. Sitting with her in Pansy and Norman's front room, I couldn't see any other obstacles to getting her sprinkled and leaving her to get on with being dead in a much better place and me to go back to normal. But I kept putting it off, and it was more than six weeks before I realized she wasn't ready to go yet.

Mercy read a story once about dead people who got to enjoy a very pleasant afterlife for as long as they were remembered on Earth; but as soon as they were forgotten even for an instant, they disappeared into nothing. The story came back to me and I thought it was obvious, really, that if Violet had clung on for dear life (so to speak) when everyone had forgotten her so completely, she must have clung on for a reason. She seemed so alive to me in that little pot, there must be something she needed to do before she was prepared to become nothing forever. I just didn't know what the thing that she needed to do was.

I didn't know a thing about her yet, apart from she was dead.

And then I took Jed to the movies.

Watching films is very high on our top ten list of things we best like doing. I could watch films my whole life long, back to back, and never feel like I'd wasted a second.

Jed likes old stuff he's seen with Norman, like Charlie Chaplin or the Marx Brothers, as well as anything Pixar and most cartoons. I signed him up at this cinema club for kids. It was there that we saw *Binky's Magic Piano*, which was this pretty old, pretty lame half cartoon, half live-action thing about a boy genius who could play anything on the piano and did concerts all over the world. Except he wasn't a genius, because it was his piano that did all the work. Then one day the piano decided it had had enough. Binky was doing an encore at Carnegie Hall and he couldn't play anything right, not even "Chopsticks," so he had to come clean, and then he woke up and it was all a dream. The End.

Jed really liked it. We were just about to leave the cinema when I happened to look up at the credits rolling old-fashionedly along, and they said, *All pieces performed on the piano by Violet Park with the Royal Philharmonic Orchestra at Pinewood studios, England.* I sat back down in my seat, and my mouth went all dry. I gawped at the screen because I knew it was her, just like when I knew she wanted my help and I knew her name and I knew she was loving it at Pansy's.

All the way home I was holding Jed's hand across roads and listening to what he said about Binky and how he wanted a magic guitar and could we have eggs on toast with beans when we got in, and in my head I was saying, I've found her, I've found her, I've found her. I knew that Violet was going to be dead pleased.

When we got in, I handed Jed to Mum like a parcel, which probably annoyed them both, and I went straight to the library to book a computer and look for Violet Park the pianist. I'd tried it with my dad loads of times; but it always turned up his old articles or stuff from when he went missing, never anything about him exactly, so I wasn't doing it so often these days.

The library on Queens Crescent is an OK place. It's in a boxy building with apartments and a weird cooling tower on top made of yellow bricks. It's pretty loud in there, considering the rules; and the toys, the books, and the furniture all get broken and stolen. Mostly it's full of people who don't have anywhere better to go, so nobody who works there gives anyone too hard a time. They speak to you like you're as good as the next person, who-ever you are. If you think about it, having nowhere good to go is just about the crappest feeling there is. I'm lucky because I've got my own room and, really, only one person yells at me at a time. But if I went home and everybody yelled at me and wanted me to be somewhere else, the last thing I would want was strangers in the library yelling at me for being there as well.

Ed's glamorous mum calls the kids on the crescent "thugs," and she pounds the word against her tongue so it sounds really ugly, "THUG," like she wants it to. Anyone under twenty or a bit poor and usually male (but things are changing) who stays out after dark is a thug to Ed's mother. I said he should tell her that we learned about thugs in history, and they were actually this amazing caste of assassins in India a hundred or so years ago. They strangled people with a long scarf with a rupee sewn into each end. It was their destiny to be thugs. They had no choice and they accepted it as their role in the order of things.[They had initiation rites and codes of honor and everything; they didn't just hang around on street corners wearing crap tracksuits and smoking dope.]

I put "Violet Park" in the search field and got 71,600 items.

And she was there, my Violet, about halfway down page 1 of 832, which went something like this.

- A book called *Violet Fire* by Somebody Park that seemed to be about the color of a girl's eyes.
- *The Violet Voice* and a load of other stuff from the African Violet Society, headed up by a lady called Mrs. Park.
- A site called Flowers Are Forever about two little girls in America called Janice and Violet who died in a fire, and a girl in tenth grade called Parker who wrote a poem for them.
- Violet Park Sneddon from Manchester, who died the year before last on September 8, aged 73.

- *Fat Girls and Plump Humpers* starring Jenny Park, Violet and Tia Lorene, which I would have had a look at if I wasn't in the library, where they have a block on that sort of thing.
- Violet Mary Park from Maidstone, April 19, age 57 (not dead).
- Violet Park, Indiana, a garden center from the company that also owns Consider the Lilies in Wellfleet, Massachusetts.
- Violet Park Barker from Blair Gowrie in Scotland (1913–1978).
- Violet's Rubber Stamp Inn at Ventura, California—accessories and lectures.
- Orlando Park, a writer, stunt actor, and horse trainer based at Violet Farm in New Zealand.
- Three Dimensional Dementia, which was about time travel or memory or something. I didn't get it.
- Violet Park, 1927–2002, a pianist on the Tasmanian Significant Women website.

Bingo.

The Tasmanian Significant Women website is proud of Violet Park in a big way.

My mum's friend Belinda lived in Tasmania when she was a little kid, and she says one of the few things she can remember is that her horse-riding teacher had a black mustache and orange lipstick and was a woman. There are no hairy ladies on the website, but there is a black-and-white picture of Violet, aged 26, like a movie studio shot.

Violet when she was young and alive.

She's looking down and slightly to the side like in a lot of those pictures, and she has this fine, slightly hooked nose in profile and long, long eyelashes, and her face is all powdered with hard shadows and it looks like cold, poreless clay. Her hair is that style that loads of old ladies have now because it was fashionable when they were young, sort of curled in towards her face and touching her collar and parted at the side, like you can tell she had it in curlers for the picture.

She's not as pretty as I hoped, but she is striking. Even on the computer printout that's still on my wall, which is rubbish quality, all grainy and gray, she's got something you want to keep looking at.

Violet was a concert pianist from Hobart, Tasmania,

and she lived in Australia and Singapore and Los Angeles and London. She got into the movies because she met someone at a party who was making a film about a deranged pianist, and the actress who was playing the pianist couldn't play a note. Violet's hands are actually in this movie. It's called *The Final Veil* and it's pretty dated, but her hands fly up and down the keys like little birds.

She's in a lot of movies from that time, or rather her piano playing is. I borrowed some from the good video shop in Camden. People say "heppy" in them instead of "happy," and pronounce their *r*'s and *t*'s and *s*'s, even in the middle of some emotional crisis. Films with names like *Cruel Encounter* and *The Flower Girl* and *Where Have All the Good Men Gone*?

I took them round to Pansy and Norman's so Violet could see them. Pansy loved it; she drew the curtains and turned the phone off (not that it rings much), and she sat on the sofa with Norman and said it was a trip down memory lane, just like the Roxy. Then she giggled like a schoolgirl, which I took to mean that her and Norm had done a bit of something in the back row, but I didn't ask. Every time the piano music surged in on things Pansy looked at Violet's urn on the mantelpiece and nodded her approval. I could see she was getting used to having her around. It was heartwarming, really.

| ten |

There are all kinds of questions that can really get to the bottom of what sort of person you are. I don't mean those useless questionnaires in the mags Mercy leaves lying around. I mean the questions that people answer one way or the other, and you can really tell something about them because of it. Like

- Do you believe in capital punishment?
- If someone offered you £1million, would you lie for them about something really important?
- Do you think people are supposed to be mono-gamous (i.e., with one partner for life, like swans and lobsters)?
- If you found someone's diary, would you read it?

The tricky thing about these questions is that you know what the right answer is, what you're supposed to say to convince everyone you're a good person. But it's not until you're in that position that you really know who you are. I'm sure about this because I found Mum's diary, and I didn't think twice about reading it. I really shocked myself.

I wish I could have found Violet's diary—I would much rather discover the innermost secrets of a mysterious dead old lady than someone I see every day, who does my laundry and kisses me good night and has no idea that I know what she's thinking. Because the person in Mum's notebook isn't Mum, it's Nicky, who she is when she's alone. She's not the person I thought she was. Not better or worse, just different, more complicated, I suppose, more real.

When I first stuck my nose in it, I didn't expect to find anything interesting. I thought it would say stuff like *pick Jed up for dentist* or *dinner with David* or *yoga 7:00 pm*, which shows how much I know. This is the first thing I read.

> When I'm not livid with Pete for abandoning me, I'm
> jealous of him for getting out first. It was only ever
> going to be possible for one of us to escape.

So you can see maybe why I read on, and why I should
have stopped.

It turns out that Mum is seeing a therapist called
Janie Golden, and one of her tasks (it's all written in a
printout stapled to the inside cover) is to write down
thoughts and feelings for discussion.

Ready for another one?

> I met Pete at a party when I was 19 and he was 26.
> He was so confident and good-looking. Everyone was
> buzzing around him because he'd just come back from
> some brink. I was so honored that he wanted to talk to
> me. I forgot that I didn't like him that much. I
> wouldn't have guessed in a million years that he
> would lead me to the life I've ended up with.

I kept telling myself to put the diary back because I
didn't like what I was reading; but at the same time I
couldn't stop, I really couldn't.

*Of course, it wasn't my honor at all, it was his. I
could have had anyone I'd wanted in that room, I
just didn't know it. You never do at the time. When
I'm 60 I'll tell everyone I was a beautiful 40-year-old,
but I don't feel like one now.*

You always forget your parents ever had a childhood,
and they admit they're wrong so rarely they kind of
brainwash you into thinking they're perfect. But boy,
has my mum made some mistakes. I get the impression she regrets every single thing she ever did, pretty
much. [Like she never really knew who she was in the
moment and only worked it out afterwards when it
was too late.]

*For every decision I make there's the other thing, the
alternative route, and I find myself hankering after
it as soon as it's gone. Pair of shoes, marriage, same.*

I never really asked myself if my mum and dad were in
love. You don't. I never looked at the root of things,
because it wasn't my job. Mum's made jokes for years
about her terrible marriage, and I just thought that was

her making being heartbroken funny. Now I don't know
what to think.

One of the kids asked me why it was called a nuclear
family, and I said it was because it explodes with
devastating consequences, which I'm sure has been said
before. I don't have an original thought in my body.

Here's something I never would have known without
doing the wrong thing and invading my mum's privacy.
When I was about nine or ten, she met a man and fell
for him. Nothing happened; but she wanted to give
everything up for him, so she never saw him or spoke to
him again because she couldn't handle what would
happen if she did. I'd like to ask her all kinds of things
like, Was it worth it? Why don't you look for him now?
Are you sure? In her notebook it says that after less than
a week she had completely forgotten what he looked like
and could only remember bits—an eye, a stretch of gum
and teeth, his hands. I want to tell her that she should
have kept on seeing him until something got to her, like
he picked his nose or was rude to a waitress. Then he
could become real and annoying like we are and Dad

was, not faultless and impossible. Then she wouldn't end up talking about him to a therapist after all these years. But if I say anything about it, she'd know where I'd been and she'd probably hate me.

My mum reckons she gets about an hour a day to herself, usually around ten at night. But she instantly forgets what it is she's been dying to do all day, so she looks in the paper at what's on TV and ends up doing nothing. For me doing nothing is pretty much the aim; but at some point that must change, because doing nothing makes my mum sad.

Mum has got quite a lot to say about us in her notebook. She sees straight through Mercy, because she's been there and done that; and she reckons that her job is to ignore Mercy as much as possible until she comes out the other side, when she will be on hand to pick up the pieces. I guess this is about sex and drugs and tongue piercing, and I think she's probably right. Mum says very sweet things about Jed, like we all do because he's our lucky mascot or something, unrattled by the skeleton in the closet, wrapped up in LEGOS and squirrels and Babybel cheese. She's afraid of the moment he sacks her as Number One Important Person in the World, and she knows its coming so she's feeling a bit clingy. She says weird stuff about me, and of course it's my own fault that it's doing my head in, because I wasn't supposed to see it.

> I'm worried about Lucas. He's turning into his dad, on purpose, before my very eyes; and he's doing it badly because he never really knew Pete, not the way he would if he was still around. He doesn't know the half of it, and I don't think I can tell him.

I have no business knowing this much about my mother.

| eleven |

My mum's got this thing about teeth. She's really strict about it. We all have to brush our teeth all the time and floss twice a day. She goes crazy at Mercy about tobacco stains. Some nights when I come in really late, I turn the key in the lock when I'm shutting the door so it's quiet, and tiptoe up the stairs all considerate, and go past her room with my shoes off, and she calls out, "Brush your teeth, Lucas!" It's like she's been waiting up all night just to say it, like she may not be able to control us anymore or even know where we are half the time, but she's never going to give up on our teeth.

Our dentist is near to Apollo Cars, above a dodgy minimarket that used to be a Citroën garage and smells very strongly of roast chicken. You ring a bell, go up some stairs, and you're there.

There's a painting in the exam room. I must have seen it loads of times before, twice a year for more than eight years, to be exact. I've looked at it and half listened while the dentist chats about something weird, like the emotional properties of flowers or the similarities between a spider's web and al-Qaeda.

But it was the last time, tipped back in the chair with my face stretched open and somebody's surgical gloves in my mouth, that I finally really saw it.

It's a portrait of Violet.

I think I nearly swallowed the dentist's hand.

It spooked me, like Violet was stalking me or something. What was she doing there?

I was thinking, Had this always been a picture of Violet, or was she haunting a different painting just to get to me? When I left would she disappear and be replaced by an ocean view or a small child with a dog?

Because that's what it felt like, not a painting at all but the real Violet Park looking down on me from the wall.

We couldn't take our eyes off each other.

She was in a wide wooden frame that made the painting look bigger than it was, which was more the size of a shoe box I suppose. I liked the painting, the way I could really see the creases in her blouse, each strand of her hair, stuff like that. Her hair was red. I didn't get that from the black-and-white photo; it could be any color in that. There was something timid about her—the angle of her head, the sideways glance—and something hard, too, like you wouldn't mess with her—flared nostrils like a horse's and a strong chin. The brush marks were thick in the background, like whoever painted it was in a bit of a rush when they got to that bit and sort of went blob, blob, blob.

But those eyes were incredible. Green and almost 3-D where the paint had been piled on and scraped about. Even though I knew it was only paint, the eyes were so real, so convincing and alive, that I was sort of spellbound.

It was definitely Violet, and she was definitely watching.

I said, once I'd got my mouth to myself, after rinsing and spitting, "Is that Violet Park?" I hoped I sounded casual to balance out the blushing and cold sweating I was doing.

The dentist said yes, and where did I know Violet

from? And I said, "From around," which we both knew wasn't that convincing considering she's been dead for five years.

Then the dentist turned her back to me and wrote something in a notebook and said three things.

"Violet lived nearby, in the green house on Chalcott Crescent. It's a self-portrait, and she left it to us in her will."

Then she told me to address an envelope to myself at reception so they could send me a reminder in six months, she said I had great teeth, and she ushered me out of the door.

I was sure now Violet was trying to talk to me.

I was dumbstruck that she left an actual will.

I had no idea she could paint so well.

I wondered if anyone from the dentist's went to Violet's funeral or if they had any idea she'd been stuck in that urn for so long right under their noses.

Violet's house is grayish green with wide sash windows. It has a big old wisteria growing up it and iron steps that go down to the basement and a black metal mailbox. It sits on the flat of a crescent on Primrose Hill, right where another street hits it, so you can see it all the way down the road. And if you were standing inside it looking out of the windows, you'd be able to see clear to the park through the gap in the rooftops. It's got to be one of the best houses around there, which is saying something, even though it's a bit rundown, the paint's peeling off all over the place, and the pipes are a bit mossy.

I'd walked past that house at least a hundred times before I knew it was Violet's.

It was so familiar I hardly noticed it, and then all of a sudden it was new and strange and I was dying to get inside. I stood in front of it on my way back from the dentist. I stood exactly in the middle with my hands on the railings and felt myself being sucked in. I didn't want to leave. I think I stared at every centimeter until it became as familiar and alive as someone's face— paintwork the pale color of a leaf's back and shedding like skin, pipes and wires a network of veins, each window reflecting a different light, including me in the ground-floor ones looking in.

| twelve |

I'd been thinking about what Mum said in her diary, about me being a half-baked version of my dad. I'd been thinking about it even though I wasn't supposed to have any idea what she thinks.

I sat in my room and asked myself the same question over and over.

Have I been remembering my dad correctly?

It's probably no accident that I hardly ever asked Mum about him and always asked Pansy. Maybe Pansy saw him the way I wanted to, half blind, without the cruel light of actual knowledge. After all, how well do mothers know their sons? I was hanging with a dead lady, not sleeping much, and helping myself to Mum's innermost thoughts; and Mum didn't have a clue about any of it. So it follows that Pansy's grown-up boy who's been missing for five years would be a near stranger to her.

And come to think of it, how well does anyone know their own mum and dad? I'm only just beginning to learn. You start off thinking they own the world, and everything is downhill from there. Parents do so many things to wake you up to the idea that they are less than perfect.

- Speak like they think teenagers speak (always wrong, excruciatingly wrong).
- Get drunk too quickly or too much.
- Be rude to people they don't know.
- Flirt with your teacher and your friends.
- Forget their age.
- Use their age against you.
- Get piercings.
- Wear leather trousers (both sexes).
- Drive badly (without admitting it).
- Cook badly (ditto).
- Go to seed.
- Sing in the shower/car/public.
- Don't say sorry when they're wrong.

- Shout at you or each other.
- Hit you or each other.
- Steal from you or each other.
- Lie to you or each other.
- Tell dirty jokes in front of your friends.
- Give you grief in front of your friends.
- Try to be your mate when it suits them.

Even with great parents, the list is endless. They can't ever win.

I was eleven when Dad left.

And now it had occurred to me that instead of missing him and dreaming about him and seeing him in crowds and turning him into some kind of mythical überdad, I might have been arguing with him, buying records with him, getting underage drunk with him, stealing from him, calling him a hypocrite, realizing he had bad breath.⌈Real things, mixed-up things, not perfect scenes of craving that go on entirely in my head.⌉

Dad didn't have to go through all the stuff that Mum did with us. For instance, my hypercritical phase, when every single thing Mum did was so humiliating that even hearing her breathe or chew or open her mouth to speak put me in a bad mood.

My dad got away with that because I thought he was perfect and he wasn't here.

And in the time he's been gone I've learned stuff about my mum, layer by layer, bad and good. It makes sense that the way I see Dad would have changed in that time, too.

So I started to believe that Mum was right about me and that we might need to talk about it. I had no idea how to go about it.

| thirteen |

It was about this point that Pansy fell off a ladder. Actually it might have been a chair; but whatever it was, she fell off it and cracked her head on the kitchen work-top on the way down. She woke up about twenty minutes later with a broken hip and a concussion. Norman was curled up and crying in the corner because he thought she was dead and he'd forgotten the number for 999. She'd been trying to close a window.

At least she wasn't going to have that problem in the London Free Hospital. That place is sealed like a fish tank, and it stinks like one, too. Pansy's ward was on the eighth floor, and it was full of old people pining for a smell of the outdoors. I went to visit her straight after school, and I took Jed with me because Mum had rushed there in a hurry and there was no one to pick him up. We walked in through the sliding doors, under a blast of hot air, and the smell hit us, linoleum—cabbage, and old-lady perfume. Jed said, "Is this a restaurant or a shop?" And I said, "Both, for sick people."

Jed's not good with elevators. He always stops like a rabbit in headlights when he's supposed to get in one, because he thinks the doors are going to close on him. Because he stops and takes that little bit longer to get in, they usually do.

We took the stairs.

Pansy was halfway down Edwin Sprockett ward, lying flat in bed wearing a violent peach bed jacket. The bed was padded around her legs, and she looked like one of those dolls with big knitted skirts that people her age put over toilet paper rolls. She didn't have her teeth in, and the bottom half of her face was all caved in. The teeth were in a cup on her bedside locker, all magnified through the plastic so they looked warped and massive; and Jed had his eye on them. There were a lot of teeth in a lot of beakers in that place.

Mum looked pleased to see us. She was having trouble communicating with Pansy, you could tell. I said if she wanted to go home and get Jed his dinner, I didn't mind staying on for a bit longer. Mum winked at me and gave Pansy this quick angry kiss on the cheek and left with Jed. She couldn't wait to get out of there, it was obvious.

I suppose relations can be a bit strained when you've both been abandoned by the same man. Mum and Pansy remind each other of what they've lost just by being in the same room. But while I watched Mum go, it occurred to me that it wasn't Pansy's idea that they weren't friends anymore—it was Mum's. Pansy didn't mind being reminded, not at all; it was pretty much what she was after. But Mum couldn't handle it. Mum wanted to forget.

I thought about who Dad was to each of them. Pansy's perfect, clever, handsome son and Mum's difficult, arrogant, absent husband. They might have been grieving for two different men.

How many versions of Dad are we all missing, me and Mercy and Bob and Norman and Mum and Pansy? A different one for each of us, and not one of them is real.

Except maybe Jed, and that's because to him Dad equals one blank space.

Pansy hated it in the hospital. She said an airless room full of ill people was like dying in Tupperware. She said it was impossible to get any personal privacy, and nobody wanted to be old and in their nightie in a gold-fish bowl. She said she never thought it would be possible to miss sheltered housing, but you live and learn.

She told me that after the fall she'd floated up away from her body and seen herself from above, sprawled out on the kitchen floor. But her near-death experience didn't impress her much. She said, "When I turned round to find that tunnel to the afterlife I read about in *Readers Digest*, there was bugger-all there."

Mainly Pansy was worried about Norman and how he was coping without her. I said him and Jack were most probably scoffing sweets and swapping war stories right at that moment, but it didn't come out as funny as I'd hoped. She said I should take Violet's ashes home with me while Norman was on his own because he'd only keep seeing them and think someone had died and get upset. I tried to cheer her up by telling her about Violet's website and her portrait, and how I found out at the dentist that she'd been practically living round the corner and everything. But Pansy wasn't really listening, and then the nurse showed up and said it was time for Pansy's bed bath. That was my cue to leave.

Because Pansy had asked me to, I went straight to see Norman, and he opened the door looking baffled and a bit tearful. The home help was over, all cheerful banter and loud whistling. I think Norman thought he might be married to her. He was struggling to hide his disappointment. When he followed me into the front room and saw the urn, he started weeping all over again. I couldn't get it out of him who he thought had died.

"It's Violet, Grandad," I said over the noise of the vacuum cleaner.

Norman looked horrified and said, "Violet? When did she die?" but I didn't have time to explain.

I let Violet have one last look around. Then I checked her lid was on tight and shoved her in my book bag. And because I couldn't deal with taking her home and explaining to anyone why I had what I had in my bag, I went to Bob's.

Question: How do you show up at someone's house with a dead lady in your bag?

Answer: You don't tell them.

While Bob was in the kitchen I shoved my bag in the

bottom of his wardrobe. Violet was hating me right now for bringing her here. I could feel it seeping through the fabric. This place was the opposite of Pansy and Norm's. There were no brass ornaments, no royal wedding plates on the wall, and no doilies on the furniture. Bob doesn't do much decorating, or cleaning even. There was a communal hallway that smelled of old soup. There was a bare lightbulb in the bathroom, candles and incense sticks, and no TV.

Violet was most definitely unimpressed.

Bob made some green tea, which he told me the Zen Buddhists drink to focus their minds before meditating. I knocked it back because I thought a clear head could only help at this point. It tasted like grass. He asked me how things were at home and I grunted a bit. Bob said, "Your mum is worried about you," and I said, "Yeah, she thinks I'm turning into Dad." He said, "Are you?" and I said, "How do I know?", which he agreed was a fair point.

Then I said something about Mum having more than enough problems of her own without inventing stuff about me. Bob called my bluff because he said, "Oh, so you're an expert on your mother's state of mind, are you?" I told him that I was because I'd found Mum's diary and couldn't stop reading it even though I wasn't happy knowing what it made me know.

It was a relief, actually, telling somebody.

Bob told me I should put a stop to it because it was a violation. He said, "It's unforgivable." He said there were ways to talk about stuff I'd read without admitting I'd read them.

I told him about when she'd written *I wish I loved Bob* because I thought it might interest him, but he just frowned and looked at the carpet.

Before I left he asked me how Pansy was. He said Mum had called and told him what happened. I told him about Pansy's brush with the afterlife and how it failed to meet her expectations. We agreed that was just like Pansy. Even heaven wasn't up to standard.

| fourteen |

My friend Ed, with the fancy mum and the house in Primrose Hill, said I've always been weird and now I'm getting weirder. He said he's always liked that I dress like an old man and talk to myself (apparently) and don't mind all that much what people say about me. But then he said I have to start minding, because the people who are talking about me are girls, pretty ones, and he wants to go out with one of them. Ed wanted me to go for a drink at some bar with these pretty girls not dressed like an old man, not talking to myself, not being anxious or wanting to be alone, i.e., not being me at all but some perfect friend who Ed wants to pretend I am.

I was dreading it.

But I went because Ed is my friend and I don't actually have many. Even though we're different, I like him.

I can't quite remember how I met Ed. He was around in my field of vision for a while before we actually spoke. We were both on our own a lot when he started school, and so we ended up being on our own together. Ed started halfway through a term in year nine. He'd been to one exclusive, expensive school after another and got thrown out of every single one. According to Ed, you don't have to do that much to get asked to leave. His mum is tearing out her very blow-dried hair about him getting such a low-brow education; but Ed says this school is the first one he's ever liked, so they'll have to agree to disagree. And of course, Ed doesn't stick out anymore like when he first arrived. He fits right in. Everybody likes Ed.

So we went for that drink, even though it was the last thing I wanted to do. It was a nice Camden evening; the sky was making up for how small it was by going pink and purple and gold all over the Stables Market. I never have a problem in pubs, maybe because of how tall I am; but we went somewhere new and Ed headed straight for the garden, just in case. I had a Guinness, disgusting and delicious at the same time. Ed was drinking trendy beer out of a bottle and biting his nails.

He said, "They're late, they're not coming," almost as soon as we sat down.

I'm not sure which one of us was more nervous.

Ed had already told me what he thought I needed to know, which was that the girls were called Natalie (blonde) and Martha (brown), and they were both seventeen. The blonde one, Natalie, was on the gym team and had her belly button pierced and was Ed's, so I was not to try to impress her in any way. I could have Martha apparently, who Ed hadn't bothered to learn anything about.

I was just saying it was ironic that Ed was all on edge and nervous (for once) instead of me, and then the girls showed up. It just floored me, because while Natalie was very pretty in a nice enough way and I didn't at all fancy her, Martha was so beautiful I wanted to cry.

That first night with Martha I did a lot of staring. I didn't take my eyes off her the whole time and she says she was grateful. She says generally people don't notice her.

I don't know how this is possible.

When Martha called two days and two-and-a-half hours after we first met, I picked up the phone and she said, "Hello, it's Martha. Martha Hooper, Natalie's friend. We met on Friday," like that, on and on, as if I knew a load of other Marthas or would never remember her. It killed me.

I don't remember much about that evening, but I remember everything about Martha.

Martha is nine months older than me.

Martha has not got brown hair. Martha's hair is a thousand different colors, each hair different from the next—black, almost black, chocolate, chestnut, mahogany, amber, blonde.

Martha's eyes are not green. They are olive and tree bark and ivy and jade.

Martha's skin is pale and soft, palest on the inside of her wrists, softest on her thighs, freckled on her nose and cheeks and shoulders.

Martha is an only child and her mum and dad are still in love and Martha's mum has got cancer.

Martha says her mum has had cancer of one kind or another for over ten years, since Martha was seven.

She says they have a joke in her house about the number of times her mum wore a wig to her birthday parties when she was growing up.

Martha says her mum is the funniest woman alive and that she can make you laugh at anything, even dying at forty-four. Her mum says the only way to deal with cancer is to mock it and make it feel small; otherwise it takes over everything you do or say or think and then it's winning.

Martha says it usually always wins eventually.

The second time I saw Martha she took me to St. John's garden, a very quiet bit of Regent's Park by the rose garden that I didn't know existed. Hardly anyone goes there. It was sunny and quiet. We sat on a blue bench, and Martha kissed me. I put my head on her lap and looked up through the trees at the sky, and she stroked my hair.

She asked me one question, a vague one. "Tell me something about yourself that nobody else knows."

This wasn't hard. I had a lot to choose from. I told her that. I said I didn't do much talking, really. She said, "You can talk to me."

So I did. About Dad. About Mum and Bob and Jed and Mercy and Pansy and Norman.

And about Violet.

"Violet Park?" she said "The pianist? My dad's got

one of her records. I watched The Final Veil over and over again when I was a kid just to see her hands."

"Like little birds," we said at the same time.

I wanted to marry her there and then.

| fifteen |

I went with Norman past Violet's house while Pansy was still in the hospital. I didn't plan to. Me and Jed and Norman were taking Jack for a walk on the hill, and we just went that way, that was all.

I was walking behind them down the road because I had Jack on the leash and he'd stopped to sniff interesting invisible thing number thirty-seven. When they passed her house, I thought I heard Norman say to Jed, "Violet's place eyes left," and I said, "What?"

They stopped and I said again, loud and a bit aggressive, "What did you say?" Norman looked back at me and Jed looked at his feet.

And then Norman said quite clearly, "This is Violet's house, the lady whose ashes you found. The pianist."

Everything went quiet, and I was suddenly very far

away and looking at Norman through a telescope.

I asked, "How do you know that?" (because really, what were the odds on Norman knowing anything about it?). He said, "I know that because your dad used to visit her here."

Norman's got this way of talking where he hardly moves his mouth and his voice is very deep and very quiet. He has a big old dappled mustache that bobs around so his hardly moving mouth and his very quiet words sometimes don't make themselves heard. I rewound to double check and heard, "Your dad used to visit her here."

I was torn between believing him and just bursting out laughing.

How could Violet Park and my dad have anything to do with each other at all?

As far as I knew, the only places those two were even remotely connected were Pansy's mantelpiece and my own brain.

But there was something about the way Norman looked at me. It was as if he hadn't been inside himself looking out for a long time. It was like he knew exactly what he was saying for once and he was willing me to notice.

So I said, "Why did Pete visit Violet?"

It was Jed who answered. Jed, my bloody five-and-a-half-year-old brother, who suddenly might know things I didn't about the dad he'd never met. He said, "He was making a book about her." He was still holding Norman's hand and looking up at him while he said it.

And then there was a pause while we both looked at Norman, and then Norman said, "Who? Who was writing a book?"

"Why didn't you tell me this before, Grandad?" I asked.

Norman shrugged his shoulders and started walking again. He said, "Before what? What are you talking about, Lucas?"

And that was it.

When we got to the park, I left them playing with the dog for five minutes and called Bob on my mobile. I didn't bother with small talk; I just said: "Do you know anything about Violet Park?"

Bob was dead quiet for a minute, and then he said, "A bit. Why?"

"Did my dad know her?" I asked.

Bob half laughed and half sighed down the phone. I could tell from his breathing he was keeping something in. "Who told you that?"

"Norman," I said, "so it could be made-up senile stuff or it could be true. I've no way of telling."

"It's true," he said after a bit of a gap. "Yeah, your dad knew Violet Park quite well."

I lay down in the long grass with the phone still against my ear and I looked at the sky (mottled cloud, one bird, one plane). I concentrated on breathing.

Bob said, "What else did Norman tell you?"

"Not much," I said. "He clouded over."

Bob said, "Do you want to come round?" and I nodded because I forgot he couldn't see me.

"I have to walk the dog first," I said.

I watched the two of them for a while, my grandad and my little brother. I stayed in the long grass and watched them from a distance.

I've said before that they liked hanging out together, but it wasn't until now that I realized what a double act they'd always been. I'd got a glimpse of their world for the first time, awash with secrets. And though I've said before that I suspected Norman knew more than he let on, I never thought I was right.

They'd looked guilty, the two of them, standing right outside Violet's house. There's no other word for the way they'd looked.

And now I understand why they stick together. I've thought about it a lot.

When he is around Jed, Norman still gets to be the commanding old man that he would have been if all those little strokes hadn't been chipping away at him year after year.

And Jed has a lifeline to his stranger of a dad after all.

I had no idea how hard it would be to filter information from a man with dementia through the mind of a five-year-old boy. Norman and Jed's combined version of anything is so garbled, it's a mangled wreck of the real event.

Jed probably knew I was going to corner him and ask him a load of questions he didn't want to answer. He managed to avoid me for a few hours by being at a friend's house, then very busy reading with Mum, then engrossed in a video he's seen maybe thirteen times and that I've definitely heard him say was boring and for babies.

It was a change, because mostly at home he hangs out with me a lot, so I almost missed him.

Finally, though, he gave in, and I got to interrogate him.

I said we were playing Good Cop Bad Cop. He gave me his police hat and he was in plastic handcuffs. I taped it.

Me: This is Officer Lucas Swain, Monday, 3 of October, 18:04 hours, questioning the suspect, Jeddathon the Howler, otherwise known as Black Jed. The tape is running. Black Jed, tell me what you know about Norman Swain, alias Mad Norm.

Jed: He's my grandad.

Me: Two master criminals in the family. What has Mad Norm taught you about the business?

Jed: (whispering) Don't call him mad, Lucas.

Me: (whispering) Sorry.

Me: So, what's he taught you?

Jed: About what?

Me: Let's start with his son, Pete Swain, the invisible man.

Jed: Dad wasn't Grandad's real son. Did you know that?

Me: He told you that? I didn't think Norman knew. I thought he'd forgotten.

Jed: Sometimes he remembers.

Me: And he told you. Does he mind?

Jed: No. He says he was a good dad. . . . He played with Dad a lot.

Me: He plays with you a lot, too, even though he's not our real grandad.

Jed: Yes he is. Shut up, Lucas.

Me: Do you want to see your lawyer?

Jed: Are you still buying me sweets after?

Me: Yes. Does Norman know where Dad is now?

Jed: Don't think so.

Me: Have you ever asked him?

Jed: No. I could.

Me: Worth a try, isn't it?

Jed: I don't know.

Me: What's he told you about Dad?

Jed: Loads.

Me: Like what? Give me five things.

Jed: His middle name was Anthony. Grandad met him when Dad was six, same as me nearly; and they went to a fair, and Grandad won him a goldfish that died. His favorite food was hot chestnuts. He taught him how to fish and ride a bike, and he's going to teach me, too. Is that five?

Me: No, that's four. One more.

Jed: He had loads of friends who were girls, but I'm not supposed to get why until I'm older.

Me: Did he tell you any secrets about Dad that you aren't supposed to tell anyone?

Jed: What, like him telling Grandad he was leaving before he left?

Me: Did he? Jesus!

Jed: No. I don't know. Maybe.

Me: Jesus Christ, Jed!

Jed: Is that swearing?

Me: What?

Jed: Is "crap" swearing?

Me: Not really.

Jed: Mum says it is. And "wankster."

Me: What's a "wankster"?

Jed: Mum calls people that when she's driving.

Me: OK. Jed, can we get back to Dad? This is really important.

Jed: Grandad says Dad was a wankster.

Me: Does he? Why?

Jed: Sometimes he thinks I'm Dad. He calls me Peter. Sometimes he remembers that Dad isn't here anymore. Sometimes he thinks you're Dad.

Me: Yeah, I know.

Jed: He thought you were Dad in the park the other day, and he called you a wankster. Can you undo these? I need the loo.

Me: Why did Grandad call me that?

Jed: I told you, cos he thought you were Dad.

Me: No, I know; I mean, why did he call Dad it?

Jed: I asked him that. He said pick a reason. Is this what Dad did for work?

Me: What?

Jed: Follow people round all day and ask lots of questions?

Me: I don't know, maybe.

Jed: It's boring. Go and ask Mercy some.

Me: Mercy's out.

Jed: Go and ask Grandad.

Me: I'm going to.

Jed: He likes tape recorders.

(Interview suspended 18:12.)

| sixteen |

It occurs to me that all most people do when they grow up is fix on something impossible and then hunger after it.

I do it about Dad, and Violet.

Mum does it about what she might amount to if she lived her life again.

Bob does it about Mum, according to Mercy.

Ed does it about getting laid.

Mercy does it about Kurt Cobain and breast implants and mind-altering narcotics.

Pansy does it about her encyclopedia salesman, her son, and about some presenile version of Norman.

Norman does it about his past, which he can't quite hold on to.

Violet's doing it past her sell-by date about something

I haven't worked out yet.

The only person who doesn't do it is Jed.

He lives in the present tense only. I don't think he's any good at all at things like the past or the future. Even today, tomorrow, and yesterday trip him up. Jed says yesterday when he means six months ago and tomorrow when he means not now. Also, when you're going somewhere with Jed, he instantly forgets that you're headed from A to B. He just spends ages looking at snails and collecting gravel and stopping to read signs along the way.

Jed is clueless about time, and that means Jed is never sad or angry about anything for more than about five minutes. He just can't hold on to stuff for long enough. Five minutes might as well be a year to him.

And the thing about everyone else in my family is, we are so busy being miserable all the time about impossible stuff that being miserable has started to become normal and strangely comforting.

I mean, how much would we actually like it if Dad showed up tomorrow and became part of the family again?

Wouldn't it make everyone a bit awkward?

It would be like having a stranger in the house, like a new lodger.

It would be really weird.

At some point, without anybody noticing, the impossible object of desire must turn into the last thing on Earth you want to happen.

The day Pansy came home from the hospital I waited with Norman for Mum to drop her off. He sat at the kitchen table folding and refolding a piece of paper. I did a bit of washing up and took out the rubbish (mostly chocolate wrappers). I sensed that if I wanted to ask Norman anything and I wanted a straight answer, now was the time. I think he was looking forward to being off guard and probably just wanted to doze in his chair and putter about with the dog like before, safe in the knowledge that she at least knew who he was.

I coughed first to break the silence.

"Did you meet Violet Park, Grandad?"

He looked at me for a second as if he hadn't realized I was there and I thought, No, it's too late; he's gone back to forgetting. Then he said, "No. It was your dad that knew her, for all the good it did him."

"Why do you say that?"

"Man-eater, that one," Norman said.

I had an image of Violet swallowing my dad whole. So that was where he had gone. "Was she?"

"Other people's husbands for breakfast, lunch, and dinner," he said.

"Not Dad though," I said.

Norman shrugged. "Thick as thieves they were, at the end."

"What end?" I said, but Norman didn't say anything.

"Did Dad tell you he was leaving?" I said.

Norman looked hard at me and said, "Do you think I wouldn't remember a thing like that?"

"I don't know, Grandad," I said, which was a lie.

"Do you think I'd leave everybody wondering and not knowing if I knew?" he said. I shook my head and said, "No," but I could tell just by looking at him that he knew he couldn't remember.

And I felt for Norman, I really did. It wasn't the same for us. We didn't know where Dad was and that was that, simple. But Norman must always be wondering whether he did know. Imagine knowing the thing that you need most, and your whole family needs most, and not being able to find it, only wondering if you know it or not.

Mum arrived with Pansy and said she couldn't stay. She drove off pretty quick, like she couldn't wait to be out of there. Pansy was shrunken and frail like a doll. It scared me a bit, the thought of her being in a pot like Violet pretty soon. Me and Norman swooped and fussed around her until she swatted us off. I went to the kitchen to make them both a cup of tea, and when I came back they were sitting in silence, holding hands across the gap in their easy chairs.

Pansy's hands looked like birds' claws. The bones stood up under her skin, and her veins were all knotted and dark blue. Her fingernails needed cutting. [She looked like she was made of paper.]

She didn't even notice that Violet was gone. She sat staring at Dad's photo on the mantelpiece and didn't see the new gap beside it.

"I never thought I'd die before he came back," she said to no one in particular, and no one in particular answered, because what could we say?

"I'm so disappointed in him, Lucas," Pansy said to me, tears rolling down her face, perfect dewdrops magnifying her wrinkles.

I hadn't heard her speak a word against Dad in five years. I'd relied on Pansy for that.

"So am I," I said.

It made me cold all over, the change in Pansy. It was like someone had broken her. She'd been away less than two weeks, and she'd come back beaten.

Pansy started to talk about funerals then. She said she knew she was going soon and she wanted a say in how she went. Even though Dad would most likely not be there, she still wanted stuff to look forward to. I promised her I'd take care of it, even if she wanted a horse-drawn carriage and a four-meter statue of a cherub for a gravestone. But Pansy wants a quiet, simple service. She wants to be buried whole (no burning) in the village in Wales where she grew up. Her mum is buried there, and her dad's name is on the headstone, too, but his body is busy becoming coal, she says, in the mine where he died. She says she wants a space for Norman there, too, next to hers, because she'll only worry if he's out of her sight.

Me and Martha talked about funerals. She says she'd like a Viking burial. This means she wants to be wrapped up in an oil-soaked cloth and pushed out to sea in a long boat. Then she wants a flaming arrow fired at her corpse, which will burst into flames and burn to a cinder before being swallowed by the water.

I hope not to be there.

Martha's dad is an anthropologist, which means he looks at how people behave in different groups and cultures. He knows a lot about funerals and says they are different throughout the world. It seems there's no end to the many ways you can say good-bye to someone.

In Bali (I think) the body hangs around above ground for a while rotting, and then it gets decked with flowers and torched. When the fire's gone out the relatives have to scrabble for bones and throw them in the ocean. It's very hands-on. And somewhere, maybe some part of China, long after the funeral, when everyone has stopped grieving and mourning, the dead person gets dug right back up again and you have a party with the bones to show you're really OK and over it. It's a good job they don't have lead-lined coffins there. Martha says that if you're buried in a lead-lined coffin, no air can get in and you can't leak out, so you turn to soup.

Martha's mum wants to be scattered in some form or other in the river Ganges in India, but she'll probably settle for the New Forest. She says, "Unlike us in the West who sweep death under the carpet, the Hindu people have a very healthy attitude toward dying because they've done it before and they'll do it again." I suppose with reincarnation, dying is no big deal, as long as you've behaved yourself and you don't come back as a bat or a dung beetle.

Martha's mum and dad are called Wendy and Oliver. I met them when I went to their house for Sunday lunch. I was nervous to start with because I've never been to anyone's house for Sunday lunch before. I probably talked too much, and I can't have been that interesting when I know so much less about everything than they do; but they were keen to like me. About halfway through pudding I realized I felt pretty much at home.

Martha was right about her mum. She made me laugh so much, I nearly squirted beer through my nose. And I would never have known she was wearing a wig. Not in a million years.

| seventeen |

I lugged my old tape recorder to Bob's, and we sat and listened to the Good Cop Bad Cop game. It made him laugh, and he said Jed was very precocious and enjoying his role as the Oracle, whatever that means—something to do with channeling the words of the gods or, in this case, Norman.

I could see he was trying to figure out how much I knew and how much to tell me. He was definitely on his guard and cagey. I hadn't expected Bob to be like that, so I started behaving like that too.

And there was one thing I knew for sure that Bob didn't.

Violet was currently laid to rest in a plastic bag inside a book bag three meters from where we were sitting.

For some reason, that felt like four aces in a card game.

I asked Bob if he'd ever met Violet and how many times and what was she like.

He said that he and Dad had first met Violet together when they interviewed her for an article about music in film. It was pretty early on, when they were starting out and took any work they could get. Bob came with Dad to take the pictures.

He said they called Violet the Technicolor Lady because she had hair the color of fire and lipstick the color of blood, and she wore bright pinks and greens and purples. Bob said they were hung over for that first interview, and they kept their shades on for as long as possible because she hurt their eyes.

He said Violet made them Brandy Alexanders at eleven in the morning and told them unrepeatable stories about the rich and famous.

They were too drunk to get much done on the article.

So they had to come back.

The second time they were much more businesslike. They only had two or three cocktails, wrote everything down, and got out the camera. Then when they were leaving, Violet looked at Dad—definitely at Dad, according to Bob—and said, "Which one of you two gents would care to take me out to dinner this Friday?"

Dad laughed and said, "Me."

I asked Bob if he could dig out any photos he had from that job. He looked at me blankly and then mumbled something about not being sure he still had them, but he made a show of looking anyway. Then he started opening drawers and shuffling around in boxes while we were talking, which made it easier to ask questions because he wasn't staring straight at me the whole time.

So I said, "Did Dad actually go out with Violet, on a date, like boyfriend and girlfriend?" and Bob said, "It would have been nicer if he had."

I said, "What does that mean?" and Bob told me that Dad kept Violet on the brink for years. He always gave her enough hope so she'd give him money or buy him a suit or take him out for dinner or something. He never said no, and he never delivered, either.

Bob said, "Your dad could say 'I love you' to a woman without even blinking, whether he meant it or not. Mostly not. He said it was the way to get whatever you wanted out of chicks at no extra cost."

And Bob said, judging by Dad's success rate with the

opposite sex, his theory worked.

My dad the stud. I was kind of impressed and appalled all at once.

"Well, how come he married Mum, then," I said, "if he had Violet to pay for stuff and all these girls on tap?"

"Your mum was a cut above," Bob said. "She was beautiful, funny and bright, and she had no interest whatsoever in your father." And he threw me a photo of Mum then, taken maybe twenty years ago. It was odd seeing her like that, herself and not herself, the same person but not the one I knew. I had to admit she was a fox.

"She didn't even like him," I said.

"Not at first, but he worked hard on it. He loved your mum, you know."

"Yeah? Right."

Bob didn't say anything to that.

I said, "So Dad married Mum, and he didn't see Violet again. Then he disappeared and she died, and that's it?"

Bob shook his head. He said, "They didn't see each other for years, and then Violet got back in touch, apparently. She asked your dad to help her write her life story."

"Help her?" I said.

"Yep, it's called ghost writing."

"He took that a bit literally, didn't he?" I said, and we both forced a laugh.

"Well, he didn't get very far with it before Violet died," Bob said. He picked up this old contact sheet and stood staring at it.

He passed it to me—tiny black-and-white shots, twenty-four of them in three rows of eight. Tiny Violets and tiny Dads, posing and grinning and wearing shades. Dad was wearing a shirt that I still have in my cupboard at home. He had dark brown messy hair like I do. He looked young and happy. I was surprised how much he looked like me. And that's when I realized.

Maybe Violet thought I was my dad.

Was that why I noticed her in the cab office, and why she was waving her dead arms at me to get my attention?

Did she think I was Pete?

I didn't want her to think that. I wanted her to think I was me.

| eighteen |

I wasn't in the mood for Mercy when I got in.

She stopped me in the hallway, all businesslike and aggressive, pulling rank.

She said she wanted to have a serious talk with me about Mum.

Mercy's serious talks usually mean she's finally woken up to something the rest of us have been aware of for months. They usually take place in her room, last about two minutes, and are a load of crap.

I followed her upstairs in a hunched-shoulders, stomping-on-the-stairs kind of way, and she shut her door behind me.

"We've got to do something about Mum," she said.

"Like what?" I said, pretending not to be bothered.

"She's depressed, Lucas; have you not noticed?"

I haven't said much about Mercy before now. Nothing good, anyway. The truth is, that's kind of how we are in real life. We hardly see each other. Maybe at breakfast on school days (except she barely eats and always disappears upstairs to put makeup on) or on the stairs or at night if she's come home and I'm still up. We don't have time for more than four words each, and most of them are sarcastic.

So, anyway, my stranger of a sister was standing between me and the way out with her hands on her hips and obviously brewing for a fight.

She said it again, but with more outrage. "Haven't you noticed Mum's depressed?"

I wanted to say all kinds of things. I wanted to say that of course I'd bloody noticed, and it could have to do with her husband abandoning her with two teenagers and a baby, her having no time off and no social life and always wishing she'd made different choices and never had any kids. I could have said I knew Mum's problems intimately through stealing and reading her diary, but I didn't say any of that.

I said, "No."

I'm not sure why. Maybe I wanted a fight, too.

Mercy threw her arms up in the air and yelled at me. "You are so selfish! Is it up to me to look after everybody in this stupid family?"

I said I hadn't noticed she was looking after anybody apart from herself, which was true but badly timed. I thought she was going to punch me.

"When are you going to wake up, Lucas?"

"About eleven," I said. I was enjoying myself. I was perverse.

"She's got that awful boyfriend, she's putting on weight, she's drinking too much, and she cries in the bathroom when she thinks we're watching TV," Mercy said. "I'm not letting you out of this room until we work something out."

"Why don't you offer to babysit for Jed or visit Pansy once in a while or take Norm and the dog for a walk or do the shopping?" I said to her in a way that pointed out these were all things I was actually doing.

"It's more than that," she said.

"Well, let's see," I said, and I was pretty angry about everything by then or I wouldn't have said it. "We could go back in time and tell her not to shag Dad, who she didn't even like; or not to get pregnant with you so he had to marry her—in fact not to bother having any of us; and what else?"

Mercy was trying to get a word in, but I was all keyed up and I wasn't stopping.

"Oh! We could go and find Dad for her, wherever the hell he is; and then she could divorce him and marry that other prick, that art teacher, and pretend to get on with her life! That good enough?"

Then I pushed past Mercy and opened the door, and Mum was standing right there in the corridor, listening.

For a moment I thought she was going to do that thing of pretending nothing had happened, which would have been a relief; but she said, "I am getting on with my life, aren't I? Who says I'm not?"

I said, "Mercy does," and Mercy said, "Lucas does," at the same time, which left us both looking stupid and to blame.

"Well, what do you suggest?" she said, walking in and sitting on Mercy's bed. She was seething. It was like she wanted to embarrass us.

She said, "Come on! If you talk about people when they aren't there, you have to have the guts to do it to their faces."

I looked over at Mercy, who wasn't looking at anyone and clearly wasn't going to go first, and I said, "You should go out more," which was feeble.

Mum smiled a really unfriendly smile.

Then I said, "You could go back to college and get a degree. You're clever," which sounded patronizing but wasn't meant to.

Mum nodded.

"You could go on holiday on your own."

"Great," said Mum, meaning the opposite.

"We could move," Mercy said.

"You should get the marriage annulled and marry whatsisname," I said.

"The prick?" Mum said.

"You could decorate," Mercy said. "You could have a clear-out and take Dad's stuff to the dump. You could rent the house out. Or sell it."

Mum put out her hand to stop us. She was laughing at us in a way that made me really sad.

"Guys, do you think I haven't thought of all those things, given that going back in time is still impossible?" She glared at me when she said that.

We shrugged, at the same time, like idiots.

"And do you know why I haven't done them?"

I said no, but Mercy kept her mouth shut and they were both looking at me. Suddenly I could see what was coming.

"Lucas," Mum said, dead calm. "Do you know why I haven't moved house or remarried or gone on holiday? Why I haven't thrown out so much as a pair of shoes or a postcard that belonged to your dad?"

I wanted to be somewhere else then. I didn't know what to say to her. Had they talked about this before when I wasn't around? Mercy was breathing easier, off the hook, and everything was down to me.

"Take a look at yourself," Mum raged quietly. "Take your blinders off before you conspire in bedrooms and lecture me about getting on with my bloody life. Do you think I've dared?"

She probably wanted me to answer, but I shrugged.

"You're a fanatic, Lucas," she said. "You're a walking shrine to your father."

I didn't say anything. Mercy was staring at me. I wondered if this was working out the way she'd planned.

I took Bob's old photo of Mum out of my pocket and put it in her hand. I'd wanted her to see it and remember how young and happy and gorgeous she was when she willingly made the choice to marry Dad and have us.

She looked at it. Then she kissed me on the cheek and said, "Tomorrow, you and me are having a clear-out and taking his stuff to the dump. No arguments."

I felt bad that she'd overheard us rowing about her like that. I was ashamed. I wanted to go back about five minutes and have her overhear me saying only good things, because people never get to hear that stuff said about them by accident. It's always a slagging off people stumble upon, and being slagged off by your own kids has got to hurt.

For a while it stung, what Mum had called me, the fanatic thing, the walking shrine. But the thing is, I couldn't blame her for saying it. She was right.

And what if I'd said then that I was beginning to see Dad for what he was? It wouldn't have made her happy. I reckon it would have broken her heart.

I was the last one looking out for him, that's the thing. Without me he'd have none of us left.

Somebody had to do it.

When a family falls apart, it puts itself back together around the thing that's missing. When Dad went, the thing that bound us was the lack of Dad, the missing him and thinking about him and looking for his face in crowds.

In a weird way, the hole he left was the glue.

It was what made us close, what made us different and in it together, I suppose.

People had to get over it in shifts. We couldn't all do it together, because if we did things might have come unstuck.

[Somebody had to be the last person to give up.

It could have been any of us.

But it was me.]

| nineteen |

If I hadn't had the row with Mercy and my mum,

If Mum hadn't decided to confront me about it being mainly my fault nobody was getting on with their life since Dad left, apparently,

If I hadn't been roped, harshly, into helping get rid of all trace of him in the house,

If I hadn't been hunched in the attic, inhaling gray dust, getting splinters and being forced to hand box after precious box of my dad's books and files and papers down the ladder to my steely-mouthed, hard-hearted mother,

I would never have found the box marked VIOLET PARK.

I am not kidding.

I tried to stand up, really fast, without thinking, and

hit my head on a beam.

I nearly put my foot through the ceiling.

Mum was going, "What? What?" but there was no way I was telling her.

I yelled down the stairs something about getting a splinter and I must have sworn, because she went, "Lucas! Jed's ears are burning." I said, "Sorry for being a wankster," and Jed tee-heed and Mum laughed with a snort.

I shook the box and something slid from end to end and clattered like plastic.

It was an old shoe box done up with tape. My hands were shaking and I was trying to pick at it with my too-short fingernails. The tape was old and worn almost-nothing thin and really stuck down. I was sweating, and the dust and the sweat were running down my forehead and into my eyes. I was swearing, really quietly, in whispers, to myself.

The tape took some of the box away with it when it came off.

I lifted the lid and there was a cassette tape in there. That was it. One tiny tape in a box, marked 1.

I put it in my pocket.

I shoved the box into a corner under a horrible, dusty old rug.

Then I passed Mum a load more precious junk that was and wasn't ours to get rid of.

Once we had all Dad's stuff piled up, for a while we just sat there staring at it. Jed was going through a box of photos, just flicking really, hardly looking, but sort of wanting to be involved. Mercy had gone out because she said she would put money on there being tears and yelling and she wanted nothing to do with it. I said I thought tears and yelling were her best subjects and she gave me the finger before she slammed the front door.

It was exhausting just looking at it.

It wasn't just paper in the boxes from the attic. It was clothes and records and cuff links and jewelry and brushes and sunglasses and a guitar and an ashtray I'd made out of clay when I was about seven.

I looked at it and I thought, It's all that's left of him.

Then I thought of him in some other place, with new records and clothes and photos and kids who made ashtrays; and I thought that he was still the same poor excuse for a man, however much shopping he'd done, the bastard.

I suppose you could say I was steeling myself.

I said we should give the records to Bob. Mum looked doubtful and wondered if he would even want them. I said there was no way a collection like that was going to the dump, so she said OK, but it had to happen today.

Mum said not to take too long. She just wanted to load up the car and get rid of it all, but I needed to check and make a mental note of everything that was going. Every time I made a case for keeping something, she got a bit more short-tempered.

I found a camera.

I found a black fountain pen with a gold nib and a mother-of-pearl handle.

I found the tiny tape recorder I needed to play the tiny Violet Park tape.

I was allowed to keep some more of his clothes (two suits, five shirts, some boots, and a fisherman's sweater).

I found his watch in a jacket pocket. I picked it up and rubbed the face of it with my thumb. I was stunned to see it because Dad pretty much never took it off, and whenever I thought about where he might be, I always pictured him wearing it. It made me go cold. He wouldn't go anywhere on purpose without that watch. I suddenly thought, Dad's dead. He didn't leave us, and we're rubbishing his good name and chucking his stuff out. I wound the watch and put it on and pulled my sleeve down over it. I didn't even tell Mum because I didn't want to see her face thinking the same.

I said, "Pansy will never forgive us for this."

She didn't even look up.

I know now that Mum didn't mean it, the whole heart-of-stone, let's-get-this-over-with act. I think she had to choose between hard as nails and mushlike jelly. Mushlike jelly doesn't do when you're clearing out your disappeared beloved's junk with your wreck of a son. So, hard as nails it was.

And maybe I should have thanked her for it, but I kept thinking there was a third option she'd not considered—the give-up option, the spare-us-both-by-putting-the-stuff-all-back-and-forgetting-about-it option. The carry-on-hoping option.

I tried to bring it up a few times. I said, "Are you sure about this?" and "We don't have to," but Mum just glared like I was confirming her worst fears about me and carried on chucking stuff in bin liners.

I was angry with her when we got to the dump. I was so angry.

I couldn't believe she was going through with it, to be honest. She stood outside with her head through the driver's-side window begging me to help her, and I stared straight ahead and didn't look at her because I was scared I might spit in her face. There was a pigeon straight ahead, hopping and dipping about in all the junk, and I watched it and thought it was going to be picking through my dad's private possessions in a minute; and I called her a cold, bitter, selfish, loser bitch and I wouldn't get out of the car. I made her cry.

In the end, the blokes in the office came out and gave her a hand. They must have felt sorry for her. They thought I was a complete idiot, guaranteed.

What did I care? I felt like somebody had died.

| twenty |

It was at least a week before I bothered to listen to the tape.

I didn't give a damn about Violet Park.

I got out of the car at the dump when Mum got back in and I made sure she got a good look at the watch while I did it. Then she drove off and I sat down with Dad's stuff and just watched it. Bits of paper were already starting to lift out of boxes and flutter about and become not his anymore. I worried that if I didn't watch they would just become trash like all the stuff around them, and I wasn't ready for that to happen. I thought about how Dad's things stood out to me, how precious they were against the other stuff my brain was telling me was junk. And then I thought about all the junk and how that was precious to somebody else, and soon the whole dump became this mountain range of neglected and forgotten treasure that I had to watch like a hawk.

Somebody had to.

After a while, the men who thought I was an idiot came out of the office and said they were closing up. It was three thirty. I know that because I looked at my dad's watch. His sunglasses were right next to me, shoved down the side of a box of books. I put them on before I left.

I went to Martha's.

I'm sure the last thing you need when you've been going out with someone for three weeks is them showing up on your doorstep like their life's ended, but I didn't think about that at the time.

She opened the door and I just started crying. I couldn't help it. Martha didn't say anything. She put her arms out and I sort of walked into them. She took me upstairs to her tiny bedroom and she didn't ask me one question. She just sat with me and held my hand and got me a drink of water and waited until I'd stopped blubbing like a fool.

Then she said that stuff was just stuff. She said that when her mum dies she could throw out every single thing that had ever belonged to her and it still wouldn't change the bits of Wendy that she was going to hold on to forever, like the time she taught her how to ride a bike, or bought her first bra, or read to her every night even when she was too old for it.

I said I didn't remember my dad ever reading to me and it was Mum who taught me how to ride a bike and I didn't wear bras.

Martha said maybe I was clinging on to all Dad's stuff because I didn't have enough good memories of him to fill the spaces.

She had a point.

| twenty-one |

I stayed at Martha's that night. We stayed up late and I slept on the sofa. I woke up thinking about the dump, and Dad's watch, and Mum. Martha brought me tea and toast on a tray.

I went to Bob's instead of school. He'd already seen Mum. She'd driven straight there yesterday, from the dump. Bob didn't look too happy to see me at the door.

"For Christ's sake, give your mum a break, would you?" he said when he let me in. He asked me if I'd called her. I shrugged and said, "Not yet."

"You're out of order, you know that," Bob said, and he passed me the phone. I must have winced, because then he got this steely, don't-play-me look in his eyes and he said, "Phone her now or I'll do it for you."

This was a weak threat because I actually would

rather Bob did it, so I nearly called his bluff. But I felt sorry for him, stuck between me and Mum, making weak threats, playing Dad's part as well as he could even though he didn't have to and he wasn't family. So I took the phone out of his hand and dialed home.

No one was in.

It's much easier to say sorry to an answer-phone than a real, pissed off, on-the-moral-high-ground person. I said, "Hello, it's me, Lucas. Sorry about yesterday. I couldn't handle it. It's not your fault. I'll be home later or tomorrow. Bye."

Bob wasn't impressed.

We talked about Mum then. I thought at the time it was funny, because I'd come over to talk about Dad but we hardly did and I didn't mind so much.

Bob started it. He said, "How much more of this do you think she can take?" and I said, "More of what?" because I wasn't ready to get into it.

Bob rolled his eyes and looked out of the window for a minute. Then he said, "What did she do wrong?"

I said, "She chucked all Dad's things on the dump!"

Bob said, "Oh, so did he want it all, then?" and I said, "No, but—," and then he interrupted me, which was a relief because I wasn't sure what came after the "but."

"It's not your mum's fault he left," Bob said. "You know that, don't you?"

I said I did, and I was thinking how ironic it was, how unfair that I'd been mad for so long at the person who stuck around instead of the one who abandoned me.

"God knows she needs something better from the men in her life," Bob said, which wasn't far from what I was thinking.

I said, "You've always been good to her," and Bob laughed that dry sad laugh he always uses when we're talking about him and Mum.

"She never needed me to be good to her. She needed you and Pete."

It used to make me proud to be lumped in with Dad like that, father and son, Pete and Lucas. All I wanted was to look like Dad and be like Dad and remind people of him. Now it was making me feel worse than useless.

I didn't want to be like Dad anymore.

We were quiet for a while after that. I mentioned Dad's records. Bob said he'd be honored to take them, which was a nice thing to say, considering.

On my way out I wanted to say something to make

Bob realize that he'd got to me, that what we'd talked about had meant something.

I wanted to say something that would separate me from my dad.

Because, for the record, I know Mum is funny and clever. I know she loves us. She works hard and she takes Jed to cool places and takes us out sometimes, too. She lets me and Mercy make our own decisions and asks our opinions like she really wants to hear them. She's still beautiful, if you ask me, but I doubt any of the crap in the bathroom ever helped.

I don't know if I said it right or not when I said it to Bob. It's much easier saying everything you want to say when you're the only one who's listening.

I was halfway home when I remembered Violet was still in Bob's cupboard. She was one of the reasons I'd gone there. I stood there on the pavement not knowing what to do, whether I should go back for her or keep walking. I was rocking from foot to foot and mumbling. People were staring, but then people do. I heard someone calling my name, so I looked up and there was Martha across the street. She motioned for me to come over, so I did.

She said, "Where are you going?" I told her I couldn't decide and she laughed again, with her head thrown back, her lovely open mouth. I had my hand in her hair and she was smiling. She was like an angel, honestly, that's how she looked to me.

We went back to Bob's and I ran in. I got the bag and said sorry for stashing it there and then went to run out again. I was in a hurry to get back to Martha, that was all; but Bob said, "Lucas, are you in trouble?" He was looking from me to the bag.

I shook my head and said, "No, my girlfriend's outside." He grinned and made some joke about me storing condoms in his wardrobe.

I was running down the path and I turned so I was facing him and running backwards, and I pulled out the urn and held it up for him to see and I shouted, "No, I've been storing our friend Violet Park," and I put my other arm around Martha and we walked away.

I think I did it because the condom joke sort of annoyed me. But I regretted it straightaway. Because Bob's face was a picture. A terrible picture.

I couldn't get it out of my head for days. What I did pretty much turned him to stone. I'm sure he would've run after us if he could move. It was more than me storing someone's ashes in his flat that made Bob look like that. It was proper shock at the mention of her name— white, drop-jawed horror, like he really had seen a ghost. And I thought at the time that the ghost he'd seen was Violet's, but it turned out in a way to be my dad's.

Martha was pretty keen on having the real Violet Park with us. She said what did we want to do next, the three of us, and I asked her where she'd been going in the first place when she saw me.

She said, "I went with my mum to the hospital this morning for another load of chemo, and I'd rather not go back to school today. Let's show Violet a good time; she's been stuck doing nothing for ages."

We got two tickets for the London Eye. It was like Violet was going to come striding out of her urn, she was so excited. We played this silly game where we had to spot all the sights in alphabetical order, A for the aquarium, B for Buckingham Palace or Big Ben, C for Canary Wharf, D for Dulwich, and so on (X and J are the hardest). After that we went on the wobbly bridge to the Tate. Violet was just crazy about the river, so we went out on one of the balconies in the wind and watched the water go by, mud beige and fast and seething. I put Violet on the rail and put my arm round the urn so it didn't fall, and I had my other arm round Martha's waist. I whispered to her what must we look like, two kids on a day trip with somebody's ashes; and she whispered back that we must look happy.

And I thought that in spite of everything, in spite of her mum being so sick and my dad being missing and a big letdown, and Violet being dead, we actually were.

| twenty-two |

I hadn't told anyone about Violet's tape, not even
Martha. I didn't know why at the time; I just didn't want
to. It was mine, I suppose. Mine and Dad's and Violet's,
at least until I knew what was on there.

I took a long time getting myself ready before I listened
to it. I pulled down the blinds in my room and made a cup
of tea. I got a pen and paper. I put a chair and a table by
the window, with the tape, the pen and paper, and Dad's
little tape player all lined up. I searched the kitchen for
new batteries. I made another cup of tea and a sandwich.
Then I got an apple and some peanuts and a few other
things just in case because I had no idea how long all this
was going to take. I spent a while making a joint because
I thought I might end up needing one. I kept thinking,
Please don't be taped over, please don't be nothing. I locked

and unlocked the door and then I locked it again. I think I was putting things off because even though I was desperate to hear what the tape had to say, I was scared of it, too. Kind of dreading it, if I'm honest.

I had to rewind it first, but I pressed the wrong button and this voice was suddenly talking midsentence. It was my dad's. It made me feel sick and cold and anxious, so I turned it straight off. I sat there staring at the machine for a while, and then I dug out my headphones. The last thing my mum needed right now? The sound of my dad's voice somewhere in the house.

Through the headphones I could hear them moving and breathing as well as talking. I heard birds outside the window where they were sitting, and cars. Someone was pouring tea; I heard the clink of a spoon against the inside of a cup.

I closed my eyes—and I'm sitting right there with them, like I've traveled in time.

All of us in one room, me and the missing and the dead.

It's book lined, this room we share, wooden floors thick with varnish like clear honey, three windows looking on to bright empty sky and the roll of the park. We sit in canvas chairs and my dad crosses his legs, right over left. He frowns while he listens and smokes a lot of cigarettes and occasionally writes something down in a brown notebook. I'm thinking about that notebook blowing open and shut, swelling with the rain at the dump, thanks to Mum. Violet's chair is opposite Dad's, their knees centimeters apart, and she's leaning slightly forward in her seat, keeping watch on his attention.

She is the wrong age. I mean, I am imagining her much younger than she would have been. I'm using the photos and the painting I've seen and doing my best, but I'm definitely way out; her voice is years older than the Violet I see. It cracks and wavers and fails in the middle of sentences. Her hands dart about as she talks, a ring on each finger throwing sparks, the nails short and shiny red. There is so much life in those hands, I've got tears in my eyes just watching them.

Neither of them notices me, weeping and grinning like an idiot in the corner. They don't look over at me once.

"Let's start with your family," Dad says. His voice turns my spine to water.

Violet sighs and says it like she's said it all before. "I was an only child to older parents. They pushed me hard to make something of my life because they never had."

"Was yours a happy childhood?"

"Oh, heavens no!" and she laughs, but you can tell she's not finding it exactly funny. "I worked hard, and I don't remember much laughter. They kept me away from other children."

"Why?"

"To avoid contamination, I imagine. They didn't want me getting the scent of rebellion."

"So you were a good girl, an obedient child?"

"What else could I be, darling? I didn't know I had a choice, until later."

Violet's laugh is throaty and deep, like she's smoked a few thousand cigarettes in her time. But she's not smoking now, only my dad is; I can hear him exhale.

"And did you blame them?"

"For the strictness and isolation? For having my first real friend at the age of seventeen? Of course I did, at first. But now I understand they only did their best."

"You really think that?"

"Yes, dear, I do. I'm sure I would have been far worse in their place."

"And how hard was it, to forgive them?"

"What? It was easy! Children would much prefer to love their parents than hate them, after all."

Dad says, "God, I do hope so," and Violet arches her thin, penciled brows at him. "Why do you say that, Peter? Do you long to forgive or be forgiven?"

I watch my dad carefully for his answer and he says, "I'm a terrible father." Just that.

I want to go over there and tell him I forgive him for the thing he hasn't even done yet. But it's not true and, anyway, I can't move.

Dad asks what is it she now understands about her parents, what drove them to drive her? She stops to think, staring past my dad and into her past.

"I've thought about it many times. It was my mother, most of all. She was a teacher, and life was too small for her, too tight all over. She dreamed of being a great actress, and at school they'd told her she would never make it, being plain and flat chested. And she'd believed them. They crushed her. But she was good; I remember her being good. She lit up the Hobart Amateur Dramatic

Society's efforts, at any rate. I saw them all as a child, rehearsals included. In fact, I thought she was an actress until she followed me to school and started teaching. It was a dreadful disappointment for both of us."

My dad doesn't say anything. He looks at her and nods and waits, so she carries on. "Father was a bank manager. He was rather formal with us. I'm not sure that he ever relaxed at home. But he loved discipline and routine, so he enforced my mother's strict regimes. He was, I suspect, a little terrified of his passionate, unfulfilled wife and his musical, solitary daughter."

"You were musical as a child?"

"Oh yes, very," she says. "I frightened the life out of Mother at the theater one day. I played a piece I'd heard only once, a minute before, in its entirety without a fault. She was checking the piano for a hidden mechanism when I did it again. I think it was a little Mozart minuet, nothing spectacular. I don't remember it at all."

"How old were you?"

"Three or four," Violet says, and I can see the grin on my dad's face in the silence.

"Three or four," he says.

"I think they wished it had never happened," she

says. "It's very draining having a child like that on your hands, an unusual child, so I'm told."

And then my dad says something so unexpected, I don't know where to look. He says, "My son Lucas is a strange child."

I'm sitting there in the room looking at my shoes. Dad's shoes on my feet, and he's saying this about me.

"Oh, good," Violet says, "let's talk about someone else; I'm terribly bored of me. Tell me about this strange child of yours, this Lucas. How old is he?"

"Ten."

That makes the tape within a year of Dad leaving. I'm trying to remember what I was like when I was ten. Was I strange?

"Do you like him?" she says. "Do you get along?"

"I don't know. I don't think he likes me all that much."

I'm thinking, Yes I do, you idiot, yes I did.

"Why is he strange?" says Violet. I can't believe she's asking about me; they're talking about me while I'm sitting in the corner, listening. I would be honored, except for what they're actually saying.

"He's on his own a lot. He stares. I think he suspects

me of something."

"Suspects you of what?"

"Later, maybe. Another time," my dad says; and the funny thing is, he's looking at me when he says it, like he knows I'm listening in.

"Do you have children?" he asks her. She frowns and shakes her head while she sips her tea the way people sip tea when it's way too hot, just for something to do.

"No," she says. "I never wanted them. I'm not the mothering kind, too selfish. I would have been stuck at home playing the piano to nobody. That was never my intention. I always knew I would never have any."

"What made you so sure? How old were you when you knew?"

"I didn't want to turn into my mother—all that talent stifled. She was a miserable, bitter woman who spent her life in the reluctant service of others. She would have considered my having a family the utmost betrayal."

"So because your mother was unhappy you decided being a mother wasn't for you?"

"Precisely. Although imaginary children are no trouble at all."

"Imaginary children?"

"Yes. In the fifties I invented a rather glamorous son called Orlando, who was a racing driver or a horse trainer or a stunt actor, depending on what party I was attending."

"You told other people about him?"

"Of course! That's why I invented him. He was irresistible. They couldn't get enough of him. What else was I going to talk about at all those parties? The key of B flat? The dressing rooms and catering at Pinewood? Orlando livened things up a bit."

My dad laughs his brilliant, all-consuming laugh, the one I can't believe I've nearly forgotten. Saying something funny to my dad and hearing him laugh always made me feel proud and smart and warm inside.

"I can't believe you," he says, still laughing, wiping his eyes. "You invented a child to have something to talk about at parties? Who was the father?"

"Oh, I wouldn't talk about him," Violet says with a smile. "I may have hinted that he was awfully famous. It raised the stakes, you see, upped the scandal. Fatherless children were very big news in those days, not like now, where nobody raises an eyebrow."

I did, I want to say. I raised an eyebrow when I became one.

My dad says, "Tell me about growing up in Tasmania," and Violet says, "I thought it was paradise, the sea and the mountains and the heat. I thought I must be one of the lucky ones, to be born there. And then I found out it didn't belong to us; we stole it from its people. Can you imagine how that felt?"

My dad asks, "Did you feel responsible?" and Violet says, "Well, someone in my family had to." Then she pauses and says, "I felt like a bloodstain on a white sheet. I felt terribly conspicuous, terribly to blame."

"How did you find out?" asks my dad, and she says, "I read it in a book. I was no more than eight or nine. I was sitting by myself on a cushion in the corner of Hobart Library. Very shiny floors in Hobart Library, very high ceilings."

"What was the book called?"

"Do you know, I can't remember? It was lying on the floor under a shelf, and I felt sorry for it so I picked it up and started reading."

"You felt sorry for the book?" My dad is smiling.

"I am a very emotional person," Violet says, and she

shifts a little in her seat, rustle, rustle. "Think how I felt for the Aboriginal people."

Violet's voice has only the slightest hint of an accent. She speaks a very proper English, quite blunt, sharp and clipped with only a shadow of down under. I am thinking about her voice. My dad must be thinking about it at the same time because he says, "Is that why you have removed all trace of your homeland from your life, from your voice?"

"Oh, I became less angry the farther away from the place I was," she says. "And I mellowed with age. Now I'm proud to be a Tasmanian woman. I just wish I had a few more native warrior women for company. I mean, what did I do? Play the piano at the movies."

"And your voice?" my dad says. "You sound utterly British."

"I had to take speech lessons to get anywhere in my business. You Poms all thought I was a sheepshearer," and for that sentence she puts on her richest, overbaked Tasmanian drawl. They laugh briefly together, two different octaves on a grand.

He asks her when she left Tasmania and she says, "I was seventeen. That was a time to arrive in London, my goodness. I came to study at the Royal Academy. Coming here was like somebody turning the lights out. There was no heat, no glare from the sun, no color. It was too strange, too depressing. I stood on Westminster Bridge and imagined the water in the Thames flowing all the way back to Australia, flowing all the way back home."

"Were you homesick?"

"Yes, very. But I learned to live with that because I didn't want to go back. I never have."

"Do you regret that? Would you like to go there again?"

"Darling, the next place I'm going is in the ground."

"Oh, Violet, you've got a while yet."

"Not if I have a say in it."

Me and my dad both look straight up at Violet when she says this, our heads snap up at exactly the same time. It's not so much what she says—a simple, throwaway comment that could mean nothing. It's the way she says it. The silence between them stretches out as I watch him watching her say that.

"What's this interview for, anyway, darling?" she asks, changing the subject. My dad says it's not for the book; it's just a profile, maybe for a Sunday paper, nothing much but he likes to be thorough.

Violet says, "There I was thinking you just wanted to spend time with me."

They smile at each other in the quiet on the tape.

"Will you write my obituary? I'd like you to do it."

"If I'm still around," Dad says, and I think, You will be, give or take a year, and then you'll fall in a big black hole. I'm wondering if her obituary might've been the last thing he did before he went, if he ever did it.

Then Violet coughs and shifts in her chair, which creaks. She says, "And now I'm tired of listening to myself talk. It's your turn. I will ask you five questions about your personal life, for my own profile. And keep the tape running because it's only fair."

| twenty-three |

If you could interview anyone and ask them five questions that they had to answer truthfully, who would they be and what would you ask them? This is one of those never-ending questions, like if you could meet three figures from history, who would they be? (Mahatma Gandhi, Kurt Vonnegut, Bill Hicks) Or what four things would you take to a desert island? (a yacht, a water-distilling kit, an iPod with everlasting batteries, and Martha, but that's cheating) Whenever you answer them, you instantly change your mind and think of something better that you wish you'd said instead. Or I do, anyway.

I'm not sure that I would choose my dad. If I could interview anyone in the world, anyone at all, I'd have a duty, surely, to get the truth out of someone more important, because my thing about my dad is only my problem but some people are everybody's problem.

But providing my dad was still alive and I got to interview him, I would ask him this.

1. Where the hell have you been since October 16, 2002?
2. Why didn't you contact us?
3. Was it something we did?
4. Any regrets?
5. What happens now?

Violet asked my dad five questions. I know them and his answers by heart because I've listened to them over and over again, trying to learn the things he said and the things he's not quite saying, if you know what I mean.

It was less than a year before he left, and you can tell from his answers he was already thinking about it.

When and where were you happiest?
On a houseboat in Chelsea Wharf, about 1985. I was with Bob at a party. We were drunk; I'd just come out of rehab and got a job for The Times. I

was about to meet the girl I was going to marry, all in one day.

What is your greatest regret?
Not meeting the people I love's expectations. I come home and they're disappointed. It's not a good feeling. That and the failure of diplomacy in international affairs.
And not knowing my real father. Take your pick.

(How does my dad feel about Jed, I wonder? I can't believe how people turn their lives in circles and repeat the mistakes that screwed them over in the first place. You'd think they were cleverer than that.)

Who have been the most influential people in your life?
Nicky because she loves me even though I am bad at loving her back.
Bob because he's always been there and without him I'd have half the memories, even though he's messed his own life up royally and worships my wife, the idiot.

*A guy called Mitchell Malone. He was a speed freak
hospital porter who nearly killed me over a poker debt.
He could have done; I had no chance. He would have
dumped my body in the river and nobody would have
known. He changed his mind and let me go. I never
knew why. He was influential, wouldn't you say?*

What's wrong with the world, Peter?
*God, I don't know. Where do you start? People give
up. We're defeatist and we stop striving or fighting
or enjoying things. It doesn't matter what you're
talking about—war, work, marriage, democracy. It
all fails because everybody gives up trying after a
while; we can't help ourselves.
And don't ask me to solve it because I'm the worst.
I'd escape tomorrow if I could, from every single
thing I've always wanted.*

(Straight from the horse's mouth. Give it a while, Pete,
and you will.)

**If a good friend asked you to, would you help
them to die?**

God, I don't know. I believe in the right to die if
that's what you're asking. I mean, if people are sick
or have no quality of life and they're of sound mind
and they want to go, then who am I to stop them?
But I don't know if I could help them do it. I'm a
coward. My friends know that about me. They'd
pick someone braver. They wouldn't ask me.

I am asking you to help me die, Peter.

That's where the tape stops. It shuts off loud like someone's fist just landed on it, my dad's, because Violet just
asked him to kill her. On tape.

It's what I did, too, punched the thing half off the
table because I couldn't believe what I was hearing.

The quiet of my own room took a minute to get used
to. I opened my eyes and pulled off the headphones and
I was on my own again, so many years later, still listening for their voices, trying to hear what was no longer
there. What did he say to her once the tape was stopped
and he'd lit another cigarette, hands shaking, while she
calmly poured more tea?

I mean, what was he supposed to say to that?

You must be joking.

Of course you're not serious.

Very funny, Violet.

No way on God's Earth.

How dare you?

Try suicide (falling under a train, jumping off Archway Bridge, gunshot to the head, etc., etc.).

Or maybe he said, *Yes, OK, I will.*

| twenty-four |

Martha's mum died. Wendy died.

People kept saying it was to be expected, it wasn't too much of a surprise, that kind of thing; but Martha says it doesn't matter how much warning you've had or how prepared you are for it, death is still sudden and it's still a shock.

"One minute she was here," she said, "being my mum, and the next she was nowhere forever. How is it better that I've known it was going to happen for ten years?"

She made me think about it, the sudden definite moment when someone dies. I saw it was what I'd been spared, in a way, by my dad's ambiguous departure. The lines around him are all blurry, the lines between being alive and being dead, like he's been slowly fading from one to the other the whole time he's been gone. My dad being dead now would still be a shock, but nothing like it was for Martha, holding Wendy's hand in the morning when she was living and in the afternoon when she was not. She said she looked down at her mum's dead hand in hers and thought, It's never going to touch me again. She thought, It's not my mum anymore, it's just a hand, and she had to leave the room and be sick.

The funeral was straightforward considering Wendy's earlier hopes for the Ganges. It was in a church for one thing, and the vicar kept mentioning God, who I know she wasn't sure about.

Martha's dad read a poem about how dying was just letting go and being free or being born even, and it was incredible because it was full of hope and made being dead seem like the coolest and most relaxing thing to do ever. In the poem it wasn't like being dead was the end of everything. It was just the end of being who you were, with all the hang-ups and memories and crazy ideas that weigh you right down when you're alive.

If you look at it like that, dying isn't such a bad option for some people.

Afterwards the house was packed out and people

were practically queuing up to say how brilliant and amazing and fearless Wendy was. There was a slide show on the staircase wall, pictures of her when she was a child, at graduation, getting married, holding Martha as a baby, looking radiant, looking sick, laughing with all her own hair. People spent a lot of time looking at the slides, even when the pictures had gone round and they'd seen them more than once. I suppose it was because they still wanted to be around her and this was the closest they were going to get.

Martha didn't like it in the house with everybody talking about Wendy and getting drunk, so we went for a walk, nowhere special. It was getting properly dark and the color was leeching out of everything. The streetlights hadn't come on yet to turn it all orange. There were people laughing in the street and pushing into pubs and running across roads. I kept thinking, Don't they know her mum's just died?

We ended up sitting on a wall outside a funeral parlor of all places. Martha was laughing and crying at the same time. She said she couldn't imagine being with anyone else at a time like this.

"We're family now, you and me, you know that," she

said, and I didn't want to feel good about what she said because it was her mum's funeral, but I did.

Martha cries a lot. She says I might as well get used to it because it'll be mainly what she does for a while, even when she doesn't really feel like doing it. She's right. We both noticed that she cries the most when she's happy, like when we're together, just messing about, or when something makes her laugh out loud. Martha says it's because the instant she realizes she's happy she feels guilty for forgetting to miss her mum.

I said just because she isn't thinking about her mum doesn't mean she isn't missing her. It's just another part of the brain doing the missing, that's all.

| twenty-five |

Before the tape, everything connecting Violet and my dad felt like guesswork. It seemed ridiculous that the two of them were linked at all, apart from by their absence. And then suddenly, listening to them talk, it seemed to me that it was exactly that, their absence, that bound them together in a way I could never have imagined in a thousand years.

The thing I knew for sure was this.

Violet asked my dad to help her die.

And then what?

Did my dad say yes or no? Because if he said yes, it changes things.

Because if you agree to help someone die and disappear shortly after, there's a good chance those two things are connected.

I've been trying to remember what my dad was like in the months before Violet died and he left us, when I was ten and strange (apparently) and probably not helping much with all my staring.

Was he thinking the whole time about helping an old lady die?

Or was he just dreaming up ways of escape?

I've thought about it a lot, and I'm guessing things went something like this.

After Violet asked my dad to kill her, after the tape recorder got switched off, after she maybe repeated the question, my dad said NO.

He might have got up and paced the room a bit, but mostly he would have felt pretty calm in the knowledge that there was no way he was going to help her however much she begged him.

My dad didn't do much for others, remember, and this was quite a lot to ask.

If you don't remember birthdays and anniversaries, if you never take your kids to school or the zoo or the London Planetarium, if giving someone a lift to the station is a major inconvenience, then assisted suicide is way out of range.

It's just one favor too far.

But what if Violet changed his mind?

It's not impossible.

How would you go about something like that, convincing someone to kill you?

You'd have to be very persuasive.

Pestering him about it would never have worked. My dad ignored such methods.

Appealing to his better nature would be hard, like finding a needle in a haystack. My dad was no Good Samaritan.

So how would Violet convince him?

Did she prove beyond a doubt that she had no good reason to go on living?

I mean, why did she want to do it? She must have told him that.

Maybe she was suffering from something that was going to kill her anyway, like cancer or heart disease or Parkinson's or boredom.

Maybe she'd had enough of living on her own, with her imaginary son and her records and her failing hands.

Maybe she promised him a hefty inheritance. This theory works because it funds his vanishing act. If he was really planning on going, a cash prize is the best carrot she could have offered.

Another thing I know.

Less than a year after they made that tape, Violet died. I'm not sure how—I'm hoping peacefully in her sleep. And my dad jumped ship pretty soon after.

That can't be a coincidence, can it?

So maybe he did do it.

Perhaps it was my dad who helped Violet die.

And if he did do it, I'm wondering how.

You'd have to be pretty careful, because clearly it can't look like murder and it can't look like assisted suicide even, unless you live in Holland and maybe parts of Scandinavia.

It was probably an overdose, sleeping pills and booze or painkillers.

But then why would Violet need my dad when she could do that herself?

Probably she just wanted him to hold her hand while she went, or make sure she was properly dead before he called anyone so she didn't get wrenched back from the tunnel with the light at the end.

I bet she was scared and she wanted somebody to talk

to, or someone there just in case she changed her mind at the last minute. Because that would be pretty bad if you changed your mind halfway through killing yourself and there was nothing you could do about it.

I don't even want to think about that.

Maybe she took the pills and then he smothered her to speed things up a bit. Once you've gone through with it, the waiting must be pretty bad.

I'm dying to know if he actually did any killing.

But he probably said no and left her to it.

| twenty-six |

Somehow, in between looking after Martha and keeping the whole Pete-and-Violet thing to myself and trying to be nicer to Mum, I lost sight of Bob for a week or two.

I might have been avoiding him.

Because I knew I'd have to find out what he knew.

And say sorry for what happened.

It was obvious to me as soon as I saw him that Bob knew a lot. He couldn't look at me. Plus he looked dreadful, like he hadn't slept since I'd last seen him, which actually turned out to be true. He was all creased up and unsteady on his feet, scratching his arse in a pair of old pajama bottoms, and I realized he'd been drinking.

Bob hadn't had a drink in years. Not since his life fell apart and he glued it back together again.

It was a big deal for Bob, not drinking.

"What's going on?" I said, and I was scared, like a little kid. Bob didn't say a word. He just turned back into the house and left the front door open.

He veered to the left all the way down the corridor and kept knocking into the wall. I walked behind him thinking, Did I do this?

"'Snot your fault." Bob breathed into my face at the door. He stank of drink.

"Isn't it?" I said.

"No!" he grunted, and he sort of shouldered open the door at the same time. There was something in the way of it (coats, piles of coats and blankets on the floor) and we had to squeeze through because it would only open a little way.

The flat was trashed. It looked like Bob had emptied every cupboard and drawer and shelf onto the floor and made a pile of stuff and then rolled around in it.

"Bob, what have you done in here?" I said. "Christ!"

"I was looking for something," he said with his eyes screwed shut, and then he shrugged his shoulders. "Can't find it."

"What were you looking for, somewhere to sit?" I

asked, because that's what I was doing.

"Oh, sit on the floor, sit where you are!" Bob waved his hands around, annoyed, so I did, shoeing aside a typewriter lid, a flyblown banana, and some pants. But then I got up again because the floor was wet.

"Why're you drinking, Bob?" I said. "What's happened in here?"

Then I stopped because I saw something familiar by the window: a box spewing out papers—a washing-up-liquid box that I'd seen Mum take out of her car and chuck on the dump. I looked around the room then, turning slowly, taking it all in. There were other things, other boxes, mostly unpacked, stacks of notebooks and magazines and stuff.

Dad's things.

Not everything we dumped, not even close, but quite a lot of it.

Bob was searching my dad's stuff for something.

"Bob, what the . . . ?"

"I just couldn't find it," he said; and he was crying, shaking his head and crying, his face collapsing into his beard. "I made five trips to that godforsaken place, on foot, carrying the stuff back and forth, and I couldn't bloody find it."

I asked him what it was he couldn't find, but I couldn't get any sense out of him. He was just sobbing and shaking his head, standing in the middle of his trashed flat, like things had gone way beyond what it was he could or couldn't find.

Then Bob poured two massive glasses and thrust one at me.

"Keep drinking," he said, "keep drinking"; and I didn't want to, but Bob drank his straight down and poured another.

Then he stared at me with his eyes all glazed over and he said, "You're nothing like your dad," and I asked him what he meant by that.

"Pete was my best friend and I loved him, but he was a bad man," Bob said. It just hung there between us, this "bad man" thing; and neither of us liked that he'd said it, even though we both had our reasons for thinking it was true.

"Will you tell me what you were looking for?" I said.

Bob said he didn't want to tell me anything. He said, "I've hated knowing it all this time."

"Do you know where he is?" I said. That would be

my worst, if he'd known all along where my dad was and never told me.

"God no!" Bob said. "Do you think I could have kept that from you?"

"I don't know, Bob," I said, and I was starting to get angry. "What are you keeping from me?"

Bob looked through me for a minute. He drained his glass again and poured another. Then he said, "I know something about your dad. Something he did."

"Something he did?" I said, like a brainless echo. I hate it when people do that.

"Yeah," Bob said. "We had a fight about it."

"What did he do?" I said.

"He said he didn't do it but he lied," Bob said.

"What was this thing he did?" I said.

"It was Violet."

I thought I was going to throw up.

"Violet?"

Bob nodded. "Violet Park. The lady in the urn you stashed here without asking."

I said I was sorry. Bob looked at me and said, "So was it really her in there?"

"Yes," I said, and then I had to ask. "Was she dead or

alive when you had this fight about her?"

"She'd been dead for three days," Bob said. "Your dad found her."

The hairs on my arms prickled. My stomach lifted and then dropped again. My dad found her. That kind of put him at the scene of the crime.

"Found her? How?"

Bob shrugged. "At home. Dead at home."

"Jesus!" I said. "How did Violet die? Was it old age?"

Bob looked as if he was standing on the edge of a canyon about to jump in.

"Overdose," he said, staring at the floor.

I'm not sure exactly what happens when you get a surge of adrenaline in your body. Your heart bangs inside you, I know that, and it feels like all the blood in your body drains away from other places like your brain and your eyes and your fingers.

"So she killed herself?" I said.

Bob shrugged. Then he shook his head. He wouldn't look at me.

"The thing is," he said, his voice thick with tears, "your dad lied to me."

"Lied how?" I said. "What about?"

"He said he was home looking after you. You had chicken pox. But Nicky was raging because he hadn't been back, she hadn't seen him and . . ."

"I remember having chicken pox," I said.

I remember Mum putting baking powder on them to stop the itching, and I remember still having scabs when I found out I didn't have a dad anymore.

"How do you know?" I said. "How do you know Dad was there? How do you know he wasn't looking after me?"

"Oh, come on, Lucas," Bob said, and I knew what he meant. My dad never spent more than five minutes watching over me when I was sick. Anyone who knew him would know it was a crap alibi.

There were several things I could have said. But I didn't.

Bob said, "Violet Park changed her will and left your dad everything."

"Did he know that?" I said. "Maybe he didn't."

"He knew it," Bob said. "We talked about it. He told me."

"And what did he say?" I asked.

"When the old girl goes, I'll be rich as sin," Bob said, and stared at me hard.

I shut my eyes and tried to think.

"Did you accuse him of killing her?" I said, kind of amazed at Bob's nerve.

"Lucas, I saw Violet the *day* she died and she was *happy*."

"So?" I said. "Maybe she was happy because she'd decided to die that day."

Bob stared at me. "That's exactly what your dad said."

I stared at the reflection of the room in the window. I traced the pattern of the carpet. I didn't want to look at Bob at all. What if he hadn't accused him? If he'd kept his mouth shut? Would my dad still be here?

"I knew Violet," he said. "She wouldn't kill herself. She loved life."

"I knew Dad," I said back. "He wouldn't run away. He loved us."

Bob didn't say anything to that.

And when I finally looked at him, he was passed out, dead drunk.

I didn't go anywhere while he was sleeping. I didn't do much.

I sat in the filth and I thought about stuff.

Of course, I knew from the tape that Violet wanted to die. Bob was working on less than half the picture, and I had to tell him. But I wondered at first whether to bother. I was so angry at him for being wrong, for maybe making Dad leave. Not telling him felt like a fitting punishment, but only for a minute.

I knew it wasn't Bob's fault, really.

I knew my dad wasn't a good man.

The idea had been hanging around me for a while, but I'd been ignoring it.

And I felt evil for thinking it.

But, really, I had no choice.

It's what you do when you grow up, apparently—face up to things you'd rather not and accept the fact that nobody is who you thought they were, maybe not even close.

My dad was definitely not who I'd been thinking he was all these years.

It wasn't because of what Bob or Jed or Norman or Mum had said about him. It wasn't even about Violet.

It was all coming from me, doubts and bad thoughts.

The voice in my head was my voice, so I couldn't get away from it.

And the voice was saying I'd known it all along. It was telling me I had all the evidence I needed.

Maybe he killed Violet and maybe he didn't. I didn't know anything.

And that's the point.

The proof I had was the exact same reason I couldn't be certain of anything I said about him, the reason he escaped all the blame and all the judgment I put my mum through the last few years, the reason I had him up on some stage for the blessed and the untouchable.

He wasn't here.

And while I hadn't given up all hope that he was dead in a freak accident or kidnapped by aliens or mistakenly locked in a nuthouse or lying in hospital piecing together what remained of his memory, I was beginning to realize it was far more likely that my dad just ran off because he felt like it. Violet or no Violet, he couldn't be arsed with us anymore. He'd had enough. And he got away with it, too.

So yes, my dad was cool and clever and funny and handsome, and his taste was impeccable and he looks good in photos; but that doesn't add up to anything.

I was angry that it took me so long to notice. I thought about how hard it must have been for Mum and Bob to keep quiet while I turned him into a hero, how many times they must have banged their heads against a wall while I went around in his suits and listened to his music and painted him whiter than white.

I only did it because I loved him.

And I thought, Did Violet come back for this, to show me this?

Did she wait in purgatory to point out what my dad was really like?

And what does it say about my dad that his best friend thought him capable of murder?

Not much.

In the end I woke Bob up and started talking.

"I found Violet in a cab office. I didn't know she had anything to do with Dad when I found her," I said. "I just wanted to put her somewhere better. It wasn't a good place for her to be. And then everyone seemed to know who she was—you did and Norman did and Jed did and the dentist did. And she kept popping up everywhere, and it was like she was trying to get my attention, trying to tell me something and I didn't know what it was. And then I found a tape with her name on it so I kept it. It didn't make it as far as the dump."

Bob looked up at me then.

"It's got Violet and Dad on it, talking," I said. "She asked him, Bob. At the end of the tape she says, *I am asking you to help me die.*"

He put his face in his hands and wept when I said that.

But I didn't know what to do with it at all.

I didn't know what to think or how to feel. Was everything better or was everything worse?

| twenty-seven |

If I'd been a proper, old-fashioned detective, or if I still had my Usborne How to Be a Private Eye kit, I would have dusted Violet's urn for fingerprints. There were eight sets of prints on there, because eight people handled her after she was dead.

Me,
Martha,
Pansy (probably moved it for dusting),
Norman (maybe working out if it was Pansy),
Mr. Soprano from the cab office,
Jawad Saddaoui, the structural engineer from Morocco
    whose cab Violet got left in,

Mr. Francis Macauley at the crematorium in
    Golders Green,
Pete Swain, missing journalist, angel of mercy,
    and my dad

At least he had the decency to organize her funeral. If
you could call it organize, because him and Bob were the
only people there.

Bob said they followed the body to Golders Green
and then afterwards they got trashed in a pub around
the corner.

My dad picked up her ashes the day after he fought
with Bob. It's on record at the crematorium that they
were collected. I checked.

So it was my dad who left her ashes in the back of a
cab and vanished, abandoning her as well as his wife, his
parents, his daughter and two sons (one unborn), and
his best friend.

I've decided you can look at it in two ways.

1. Violet asked my dad to help her die and broke his heart. He said no, but she persuaded him that it was what she wanted and without him she would have to do it alone. He helped her because he cared about her and the strain of it pushed him to breaking point. Then his best friend accused him of murder and he realized nobody would believe him and he could end up in jail for helping her. So he cracked and had to get out, away from everything, away from us. You read about people doing it for less.

In other words, he was a good person who did something brave and selfless and couldn't handle the consequences.

2. Helping Violet die was his ticket out of here—help an old lady, get a new life. My dad didn't do it for Violet; he didn't give a damn about her, really. He did it for what she promised him in return (enough

money to get a new identity), and his conscience
didn't bat an eyelid.

This makes him a self-serving, cold-hearted, borderline sociopath.

I can't decide between them or any of the gray areas in between, and in the end I suppose it doesn't matter either way.

He did what he did. She got what she wanted. He left.

Those are the things that count.

| twenty-eight |

Violet was waiting when I got home from Bob's. It was four in the morning. I let myself in and didn't make too much noise on the stairs and even my breathing sounded too loud, and I locked my bedroom door behind me and got her out from under the bed. Her urn was so beautiful. The grain in the wood was intricate and clear, the polish was smooth and flawless in my hands. Did my dad think the same thing when he chose it? Or did he pick the cheapest thing in the brochure and never noticed how it shone?

I sat with her on the floor while the birds woke up and the sky turned a watery gray and people got in their cars and tried to start them.

Violet had spent five years in that urn for a reason. I'd started off wondering why she picked me to help her, what she wanted. I'd thought about her funeral, her will, about finding her the right resting place. I'd thought she wanted me to solve something for her. I didn't know she was doing something for me. I hadn't expected for a minute that she was going to lead me to my dad.

I was sorry that she'd decided to have enough of living.

I hugged her in her exquisite, cold, wooden container, and I wished that I'd been able to know her when she was still alive.

We flung her ashes in the Thames. I remembered what she said on the tape, that when she was homesick she imagined the water flowing all the way back home; and I thought she could go home that way if she wanted, or really anywhere if she didn't. The wind threw most of her back in our faces, me and Martha and Bob.

On the way home I felt sad and tired and empty, like she'd only just died. The urn was so different without her in it.

I hope she ended up where she wanted. I hope she found what she came back for.

I hope I was some help, walking into that cab office out of my mind.

And I suppose that's why I had to tell somebody, why I had to write things down.

I wanted to add to what she'd left behind—a handful of movies, a portrait, a contact sheet, and a tape.

Violet changed my life and I wanted to stop hers from turning to nothing.

| twenty-nine |

Bob said something to me the other day.

He said that if Dad did it for the money, I could take comfort in the fact that she didn't leave him everything after all.

I said, "What do you mean?" or "How do you know?" or something, and I was thinking about the portrait she left the dentist, because that was in her will.

And Bob said that he read an obituary about a month after she died, a long and fawning one written by a music librarian at York University. The obituary said that Violet was survived by her only son, who inherited her entire estate, including houses in Australia, New Zealand, London, and the U.S.

"She didn't have a son," I said.

"Yes, she did," Bob said. "And I remember his name

because it was unusual. It was Orlando."

I felt sick with rage and excitement, because Violet invented Orlando Park. I knew that from the tape, and so did my dad.

Suddenly, after loving him and looking after the hole he'd left and trying to grow up without him, I knew where Dad was.

And I knew he wasn't dead, the bastard.

He was rich as sin, however rich that is, living off Violet's money in the sun.

I went to my room and I punched a hole in the wall, but I didn't cry.

I felt weirdly happy. Angry happy.

And I did something that I didn't tell anyone about—not Bob, not Martha, definitely not my mum. I can't work out if it's the start of something or the end of it, and I'm trying to stop my brain from going there. I did it and I'll wait and see what happens before I tell anybody.

I sent a parcel to Orlando Park at Violet Farm, Turungakuma, South Island, New Zealand. I found him on the Internet. He'd been there the first time, the time I'd checked for Violet. I'd looked straight through him.

I sent him Violet's empty urn, the one he'd collected from the crematorium and left in the back of a cab.

And I stuck a little note on it, round the other side from Violet's name.

It said

PETE SWAIN
1958–2002
RIP

Who knows if I'll hear anything back? It seems unlikely.

Thanks to Violet, that matters a hell of a lot less than it used to.

EXTRAS

me, the missing, and the dead

How This Book Came About

An Interview with Jenny Valentine

A Sneak Peek at Jenny's second book, *Broken Soup*

How This Book Came About

I'm betting that none of you have met a dead old lady. You might have known some old ladies who have died. But I'm pretty sure that you didn't meet one after they were dead. I know I haven't. But the boy in my book did. The boy, called Lucas, found a dead old lady's ashes in a minicab office. And the dead old lady's ashes changed his life.

Some of you might think that finding a dead old lady's remains in a minicab office is a ridiculous place to start a story. You might be saying to yourself "that would never happen." But strangely enough, it's the only part of Me, the Missing, and the Dead that's actually true.

And because it's ridiculous and impossible and true, all at the same time, I thought it was as good a way to start a story as any.

I used to work in a whole food shop called SESAME in Primrose Hill, London. I met a lot of very interesting people. Some of them were creative and artistic, some clever, some funny, some properly crazy, some a mixture of all of those things. A lot of them were old. There was a retirement place nearby, overlooking the park. Many of our customers came from there. I hadn't made friends with any old people before. I hadn't paid them much attention.

But that's where I met the real Violet Park. The real dead old lady in an urn. She was alive when I met her, of course. Her name was Eileen. Eileen was a pianist before she got old and her fingers swelled and bent in funny ways and refused to do as they were told. She had a shock of dyed red hair, always pure white at the roots. She had dyed her hair so many times it was starting to disappear. You could see the hidden skin of her scalp showing through when she looked down to study the coins in her purse. Eileen used to buy one or two eggs, a half-carton of milk, sometimes a lemon and a loaf of bread. Old lady shopping.

Eileen's eyes were starting to fail her, and she carried glasses in her pocket that looked like the bottom of bottles. Her glasses made her eyes look bigger than her fists when she put them on, which is why she didn't wear them. She carried them in her pocket, because she cared how she looked and she didn't want to look a fool. And because she didn't wear her glasses, she also carried a white stick. She wore ridiculously high-heeled shoes for someone who carried a white stick, but the stick was less medical necessity, more attention magnet, just like the shoes I suppose. She used her white stick mainly for hitting parked cars if she thought they were in her way. And for shaking at people in the street if she didn't like the look of them.

Because she was always armed with her white stick, she was always ready for a fight. She'd look like she was thinking up something rude and obnoxious and devastatingly clever to say to you, and she often was. If you said something funny in return, she'd point her white stick right at you, inches from your nose, like the beginning of a fencing match. Like a sword fight.

Eileen loved the boys.

She'd wink at our boss, Peter, who at 50 was about 32 years her junior. She laughed wildly at his jokes, like they were at a drinks party. She pretended to read trendy French literature in the local café to attract the young students and intellectuals. If that didn't work, she'd put her white stick to use and trip them up. And flutter her eyelashes and smile.

She was the first disgracefully behaved old lady I had ever met and I thought she was brilliant. She made me realize that old people are no different from young people, apart from the wrinkly skin. Sure, some old people are stuck in their ways and a bit boring and unadventurous. But so are some kids. Old people can be just as rebellious and inventive and lively and outrageous as you.

Then Eileen died. She was cremated. I don't know who was there or who collected her afterward. Her ashes were put on a shelf in an office up a cobbled alley opposite the shop. I wasn't working there anymore. I had moved away. But I heard about it and I thought about her and what an extraordinary place it was to be laid to rest. It wouldn't have suited her at all.

I hadn't known that much about her when she was alive. So just like Lucas does in the book, I tried to find out more about Eileen on Google. I got my wires crossed. I found a Tasmanian pianist named Eileen Joyce who toured Britain during World War II and

4

played on old films like *Brief Encounter* and *The Seventh Veil*. One website said she was noted for matching the color of her dress to the composer of the concerto. That sounded like Eileen to me. But it wasn't. My Eileen hadn't been from Tasmania and she hadn't been famous and suddenly I wasn't even that sure if she had even been a pianist. But while I was tying myself in knots over two dead Eileens, Violet Park was made. A boy called Lucas found her. They had this weird friendship that you couldn't really explain, especially because one of them was dead. They helped each other out. And they turned into this story with a ridiculous, impossible, and completely true beginning.

There are other people in the book that I borrowed from real life. Lucas's grandparents are basically mine. My granny really did talk about her husband as if he were the dog. And about the dog as if he were her husband. My grandad really did suffer these tiny, unnoticeable strokes in his brain, so that he couldn't tell you what happened yesterday, but he could remember WWII in minute detail. And he ate chocolate until he felt sick.

Lucas's little brother, Jed, is based on a little boy I used to help teach. Every day on our way to the lunch hall, at the exact same turning on the stairs, he'd tell me a really rubbish joke he was proud of. A different one every day for a whole term, which is something, if you think about it.

That's what happens if you write stories. You store people and events and other things until you can use

5

them later. You juggle them around and out they come, happening to someone else.

But you also make things up.

I made up Lucas's stroppy big sister, Mercy; his Mum; Nick; and his missing dad, Pete. I made up his best friend, Ed, and his lovely girlfriend, Martha.

One of the best things about writing the book was Lucas. I had my place to start and my dead old lady, and Lucas jumped onto the page fully formed, from the moment I started, like someone I really knew, even though I made him up.

It sounds silly, but I promise it's true. I learned things about him as we went along. Like he's tall and shambly and a bit odd. And alone a lot, but he really doesn't mind. That he has one good friend but no idea why he likes him. That he worries about everything. But actually he's very brave. And thoughtful. And a bit interested in being sad.

Maybe it's easy for Lucas to be sad, with his dad missing. Because he has no idea where he is or what he's up to, or even if he's dead or alive, how can Lucas help thinking about his dad all the time? About the gap that his dad left, and what it's doing to the rest of his family. Lucas thinks a LOT.

Lucas's dead old lady and his missing dad are joined together in a way that takes Lucas completely by surprise.

And here's a secret: It took me by surprise too. Because when I started writing this book, I had absolutely no idea of what was going to happen. I'd always wanted to write a book. I wrote one when I was ten, which I'm sure was pretty awful and I've thankfully lost it. I tried a few times to map out story lines and achieve a beginning, a middle, and an end like you're supposed to. But I was really bad at it. And it wasn't any fun.

And then I read something in one of those books that supposedly tell you how to write (and that I vowed I'd never read), and it was like opening a door. The book was called *On Writing* by Stephen King. He's written a lot of scary books, and I don't know about you but I'm not good with scary. I read one called *The Shining*, and it worked. I was scared. And I didn't like it. But in this book on writing, he said that if you know what's going to happen next then so does the reader. And this lightbulb went on in my head and I thought, I can just start and see what happens. And I did. And I got very excited because it worked.

I'm not going to start preaching death to beginnings, middles, and ends because it might not work for everybody. But it worked for me.

An Interview with Jenny Valentine

What is a typical day of writing like for you?
Well, it's not every day because I work in a shop two or three days a week. I walk the dog first, otherwise he pesters me, and anyway the fresh air clears my head. Then I make tea, and I take snacks to my study so I have no excuse to leave. . . .

My house is cold in winter, so sometimes I'm forced to do some housework just to keep warm! A writer's day is littered with distractions. That's how I know if something's going well—I'm not distracted.

Do you share early drafts of your books with family members or friends for feedback?
My poor husband, Alex, read Me, the Missing, and the Dead about twenty times. With Broken Soup, we cut it down to about six. My latest book, I showed to him when it was finished.

What part of the writing process do you enjoy the most (research, creating the first draft, revising)?
I love it when characters take off and start writing themselves.

What is the hardest part about writing?
Plotting. I can't do it! I start with a beginning and then I wander through the fog for a while, and then an ending comes to me. There's always a bad moment when I think, "What if one doesn't?"

When did you first realize you wanted to be a writer?
I was maybe nine. My mother bought me a book that looked like a novel on the outside but was just an empty notebook on the inside. I filled it with stories.

What would you say is the biggest influence in your writing?
All the books I've ever read. And all the people I watch. And how it felt to be a teenager.

What do you do to relax?
Walk my dog, do a Sudoku, have a glass of wine, go swimming.

What advice do you have for young aspiring writers?
Read.

What question are you never asked in interviews but wish you were?
How about, "Would you like a glass of champagne?"

What are you working on now?
I've just finished my third novel, called *The Ant Colony*, about a house and the people who live in it. I'm also writing a book for younger readers about two sisters. It's called *Iggy and Me*.

Read on for a sneak peek at Jenny Valentine's second novel,

Broken Soup

It wasn't mine.

I didn't drop it but the boy in the line said I did.

It was a negative of a photograph, one on its own, all scratched and beaten up. I couldn't even see what it was a negative of because his finger and thumb were blotting out most of it. He was holding it out to me like nothing else was going to happen until I took it, like he had nothing else to do but wait.

I didn't want to take it. I said that. I said I didn't own a camera even, but the boy just stood there with this "I know I'm right" look on his face.

He had a good face. Friendly eyes, wide mouth, all that. One of his top teeth was chipped; there was a bit missing. Still, a good face doesn't equal a good person. If you catch yourself thinking that, you need to stop.

All my friends were cracking up behind me. The girl at the counter was trying to give me my change and everybody in the line was just staring. I couldn't think why he was doing this to me. I wondered if embarrassing strangers was one of the ways he got through his day. Maybe he walked around with a pile of random stuff in his pockets—not just negatives but thimbles and condoms and glasses and handcuffs. I might be getting off lightly.

I didn't know what else to do, so I said thank you, who knows for what, and I went red like always, and I made a face at my friends like I was in on the joke. Then I shoved the negative in my bag with the oranges, milk, and eggs, and he smiled.

All the way home I got "What is it, Rowan?" and "Let's see" and "Nice smile"—a flock of seagulls in school uniform, shrieking and pointing and jumping around me. And I did my usual thing of taking something that's just happened apart in my head until it's in little pieces all over the place and I can't fit it back together again. I wanted to know why he'd picked me out of everyone in the shop, and whether I should be glad about that or not. I thought about what he said ("You dropped this . . . no really . . . I'm sure") and what I did (act like a rabbit in headlights, argue, give in). I was laughing about it on the outside, feeling like an idiot on the quiet. I had no idea something important might have happened.

My name is Rowan Clark and I'm not the same person as I was in that shop, not anymore. The rowan is a tree that's meant to protect you from bad things. People made crosses out of it to keep away witches in the days before they knew any better. Maybe my mum and dad named me it on purpose, maybe not, but it didn't do much good. Bad things and my family acted like magnets back then, coming together whatever was in the way.

When I got home with the shopping, I forgot about the negative because there was too much to do. Mum was asleep on the sofa while Stroma watched *The Fairly OddParents* with the sound off. Stroma's my little sister. She was named after an island off Scotland where nobody lives anymore. There used to be people there until 1961 and one of them was someone way back in my dad's family. Then there was just one man in a lighthouse until they made the lighthouse work without the man and he left too. That's what Stroma and her namesake have in common, getting gradually abandoned.

Jenny Valentine worked in a food shop for fifteen years, where she met many extraordinary people and sold more loaves of organic bread than there are words in this book. She studied English literature at Goldsmith's College, which almost put her off reading but not quite. Jenny is married to a singer/songwriter and has two children. She lives in Hay on Wye, England. *Me, the Missing, and the Dead* is her first novel, which was published in the UK under the title *Finding Violet Park*.

For exclusive information on your favorite authors and artists, visit www.authortracker.com.

Broken Soup
Jenny Valentine

Positive... negative... it's how you look at it.

"One of this year's unmissable reads."
—The *Guardian* (UK)

Mum and Dad moved us to a new school because they thought it was better. They gave us swimming lessons and cycle helmets and self-defense classes and a balanced diet. They promised us five grand on our twenty-first birthdays if we never smoked.

And still one of us died.

What can I say? Death is just one of those things you can work out a thousand different ways of avoiding, but you're going to meet head-on regardless.